BEATING UP
DANIEL

ST. ELIZABETH SCHOOL
50 Adler Dr., Box 21036
Zehrs Postal Outlet
Cambridge, Ont. N3C 4B1

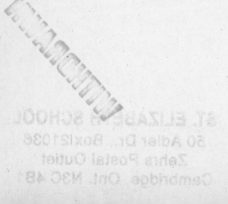

BEATING UP DANIEL

DANIEL

A.D. Fast

Vanwell Publishing Limited

St. Catharines, Ontario

*This book is a work of fiction. Names, characters, places, and incidents
are the product of the author's imagination. Any resemblance to actual
persons, living or dead, is entirely coincidental.*

Vanwell Publishing Limited   **In the United States**
P.O. Box 2131   P.O. Box 1207
1 Northrup Crescent   Lewiston, NY
St. Catharines, ON   USA 14092
Canada L2R 7S2
sales@vanwell.com
1-800-661-6136

Produced and designed by Tea Leaf Press Inc.
www.tealeafpress.com

Design: Jane Lewis
Editorial: Kate Calder, Heather Levigne,
          Jane Lewis, and Hannelore Sotzek

Printed in Canada

National Library of Canada Cataloguing in Publication

Fast, April, 1968-
    Beating up Daniel / April DeAnne Fast.

(Bayview High)
ISBN 1-55068-120-6
ISSN 1702-0174

    I. Title. II. Series.

PS8561.A84B42 2002   jC813'.6   C2002-901214-7
PZ7

To my brother and sister-in-law,
David & Heidi Wilcox,
and to Kayla, Sarah & Evan.

You have no idea how happy I am
to have you in my life.

chapter 1

pain in the neck

Blood dripped down Justin's chin. He pulled his black cape around his shoulders. He looked around for his next victim. Slowly, he walked toward the sleeping Jessica. Her head was turned to the side. He looked at her white neck and smiled. Creeping toward her, he opened his mouth. His large fangs were ready for flesh. Just as he was about to bite, he felt a sharp pain. With the wooden stake stabbed in his back, Dracula fell to the floor.

The sound of clapping filled the room.

Justin stood up and looked out at the audience. Jessica sat up in the fake bed. It was made out of cushions and a sleeping bag. Mr. Thomas turned on the classroom lights. The students adjusted their eyes to the light.

Justin was nervous. It was early April, and this play counted for twenty-five percent of his final mark in drama class. He and Jessica had practiced the play all week. Now it was Friday, and he had skipped his first class to set up for the big day. All that work was over in one hour.

The other drama students sat on rows of benches like bleachers. The benches looked like a really wide set of black stairs. The classroom walls were painted black. The windows had heavy curtains. When the main lights were off, the room was pitch black. Spotlights pointed at the classroom floor, which became a "stage" for class plays.

Mr. Thomas walked down the bleachers to the floor. He had a clipboard in his hand. "Very well done," he said. The class was still clapping. "I like how you wrote your lines," he said to Justin and Jessica. "The set design was good. I would think again about the lighting for the final scene. It was hard to see the victim," Mr. Thomas added.

Mr. Thomas was an actor. That's what he told his students. He insisted that literature and drama were the most important courses his students would take. This year, Mr. Thomas was also teaching geography. Justin joked with him about it. He could joke around with Mr.

Thomas. There weren't many teachers like him. Mr. Thomas had long, brown hair that he wore in a low ponytail. He always wore jeans and sandals with socks to school. Mr. Thomas was one of the coolest teachers at Bayview High.

"Does anyone else have comments about the play?" he asked. A few of the students talked about the costumes. James McMath mentioned that Justin could have said some of his lines a little differently. Overall, the play went over well with the other kids. Justin was sure he was getting a good mark.

The bell rang for the next class, and everyone filed out of the dark room. Justin stayed behind to clean up. His next period was lunch anyway.

Justin took off his cape, grabbed a cloth, and wiped the fake blood off his face. Then he grabbed a broom and started sweeping the floor.

"That was great! You didn't even smile when John burped in the middle of the scene," Jessica said. She was putting away some of the props they used for the play. There were chairs, lamps, empty water bottles, and, of course, the big, wooden stake.

"By the way, John, that burp was Academy Award material," she added.

John was laughing in the corner of the room.

"What? That was method acting," he said.

"You don't even know what method acting is!" Justin answered. He threw a football across the room so John could put it in the "set" closet.

Justin walked over to the costume area and washed his face in the sink. He looked into the mirror and combed his short, brown hair. Then he rubbed his chin. Still no beard. *What is taking so long?* he wondered.

Justin watched as Jessica fixed her hair. She took out her ponytail and shook her head. Jessica's long blond, wavy hair fell down around her shoulders.

"What is this, a shampoo commercial?" Justin said as he walked by her. He picked up his books from the bench.

"Don't hate me because I'm beautiful!" she answered. She pretended to pose for a camera. "Listen, Justin Andrews, you have to be at drama club on time next week. We have to get that scene right if you want to be cast for the spring show."

The spring show was a big deal. Drama, music, dancing—it was really popular in the city, and the school spent a lot of money on it.

"Yes, madam. Will our star be giving any other orders?" he asked, laughing.

"Yes, I order that you change your outfit before next class. You look like a cross between a rocker and a my dad trying to look hip." He was still wearing a black turtleneck shirt with black running pants and black shoes. He had to wear all black for their play. As Dracula, he had to be hidden in the dark.

Justin laughed. His jeans and shirt were in a locker in the change room. He was going to change anyway. Jessica smiled and turned to leave. Justin stood there and watched her as she walked out of the classroom.

"Snap out of it, buddy. She might hang out with us for class projects, but that girl has her eye on bigger fish," John said. He stood beside Justin with his arms crossed. They watched Jessica stroll down the hall toward the cafeteria. She caught up with her group of friends. The girls giggled loudly as they made their way down the hall.

"John, get a grip. I don't like Jessica. I mean, she is fine, but I know she wouldn't go out with a guy like me. Besides, I can't compete with those guys," he answered. He nodded toward Travis, Dave, and Tom. They were joking around outside the library. Those guys pretty much ruled grade eleven. They all had cell phones in their backpacks. Wherever they went, a group of girls was sure to follow. They were seventeen, and they were cool.

Justin was really enjoying grade ten so far. He had taken drama class in grade nine and liked it. This year it was even better. Mr. Thomas was a great teacher, too. Before Justin knew it, he was part of the drama club. It didn't get in the way of track-and-field practice at all, either. He could practice long jump whenever he wanted and belong to the drama club.

Justin and John headed off down the hall to change. As they passed the library, Travis looked at him and laughed.

"Hey, Justin, nice outfit," he called. Dave and Tom laughed.

"Yeah, yeah," Justin said. He faked a laugh.

"Oh, and John, the chess team was looking for you. They're one geek short for their big match. Better go and find them," Dave called.

John laughed and shrugged it off. John Case was tall and fit. The football coach was always trying to get him to join the team. John wasn't into football. He preferred the drama club, the chess club, and the cross-country running team. When the older guys bugged him, he took it as a sign of friendship. It didn't bother him a bit, but it bothered Justin.

"What's their problem?" Justin asked, looking over at Travis, Dave, and Tom. He opened the change room door and walked over to his locker.

"Why do you let it bug you so much?" John answered. "They always pick on someone. Today it's me. Who cares? When you are as smart as me and you play chess, you have to expect some teasing."

"It's not even really Dave and Tom who are the problem. It's Travis. Ever since he came to Bayview this year, he has been a jerk," Justin said. "He should have stayed at Lincoln." Justin was amazed that such a popular guy could be such an idiot. "Did you know that his father is a heart surgeon?"

"Yeah," John answered. "Too bad he didn't get his father's brains." They both laughed. When they were dressed and ready to go, they closed their lockers and turned for the door.

The door whipped open. A guy with messy, sandy-brown hair flew in. He ran for a locker close to the showers.

"Hey, John," he called as he opened his locker. He kicked off his running shoes and pulled off his sweat shirt.

"Hey, Daniel. Running on your lunch again?" John asked. Daniel always went for a run during his lunch period. He was on the cross-country team and wanted to keep in shape.

"Man. One of these days I'll either get kicked out of math or get kicked out of gym. One or the other," Daniel laughed. He was medium height and very muscular. He was built for weight lifting, not running. But he trained hard for cross country anyway. He was also the smartest guy—and the nicest guy—in grade eleven.

"With your marks, I doubt they'll kick you out," John called over his shoulder as he opened the change room door. "See you at chess!"

"Yeah. See ya!" Daniel called from the shower.

"Who is he?" Justin asked as they walked down the hall.

"New guy. His name is Daniel. He is a really good guy. He joined the chess club last month. You should see the guy play," John answered, checking his hair in the window as he walked by. He opened his lunch bag and munched on a ham sandwich as they walked down the hall.

By the time they finished cleaning up the room and changing their clothes, lunch period was over. Justin ran into geography class ten minutes late. The class was getting a new project that day. He was excited to find out who his project partner would be.

When he got to class, he wished he never bothered showing up.

chapter 2

stuck with
a meathead

Justin opened the door to geography class, nodded at Mr. Thomas, and went to his desk. Mr. Thomas knew Justin would be late after cleaning up from the play. Mr. Thomas had already told the class who they would be teamed up with for the project. Justin would have to wait until later to ask Mr. Thomas.

Justin opened his book and tried to figure out what the class was doing. For some reason, Travis was sitting beside him. Travis was in grade eleven, but he took grade ten geography. Normally, being behind a year in geography wasn't that funny. But having no idea where Canada is on the map—now, that was funny.

The week before, the students were divided into teams. Mr. Thomas asked them questions.

Some were hard, and some were easy. When it was Travis's turn, things got interesting.

Mr. Thomas asked Travis to point out Canada on a huge, colorful map. Travis strolled up to the front of the class like he knew everything. Then he pointed to Florida, which definitely was as far away from Canada as you could get! It was the single most hilarious moment in the history of geography class.

Usually, Travis sat at the back of the class and slept with his eyes open. Now he was sitting up tall near the front of the class, right beside Justin. Marvin Woods usually sat there. Marvin was nowhere to be seen. Justin hoped Marvin wasn't forced out of his spot.

"Justin, how's it going?" Travis whispered.

"Uh, fine...I guess," he answered. He wondered if Travis had forgotten about making fun of him and John earlier.

"So, I guess we're partners, huh?" Travis whispered loudly again.

Mr. Thomas looked at them and said *"SHHHHH!"* Justin sat facing the blackboard.

This can't be happening, Justin thought to himself. *I cannot be doing a major term project with a meathead.*

Mr. Thomas left the geography room to find a projector.

Justin turned to look at Travis. *"We* are on a project? What do you mean?" he leaned over and asked Travis.

"You and me—we're partners. Mr. Thomas thought we would be a good team," Travis answered. He reached into his pocket and searched for something. Then Travis pulled out a tiny bottle of breath spray and squirted it into his mouth.

Justin jumped out of his seat and hurried out the door. He bumped into Mr. Thomas walking back toward the class.

"Hey, you just got here. You're not leaving already, are you?" Mr. Thomas asked. Justin stood in front of him.

"No, I was looking for you," Justin said. "Why am I stuck doing a huge project with Travis? I might as well do it by myself. Don't we have a say in who our partner will be at all?"

"Justin, sometimes life throws you challenges. Travis needs a hand, and you always manage to do a good job. He requested you as a partner. I said we would give it a try. I have faith that you will do a great job," he answered.

"He asked to do the project with me?" Justin asked Mr. Thomas.

"Yes, and I think you should give him a chance," Mr. Thomas answered.

Suddenly Travis Armstrong wants to be partners with me? he thought to himself. He shook his head. *This is going to be a nightmare.*

They walked back into the classroom, and Justin sat down. He couldn't believe that he was stuck with Travis. Talk about bad luck.

Mr. Thomas gave the class some time to decide on a topic for their project. They had one week to hand it in. The outline was due on Monday. Justin flipped through some books on his desk and wrote down a few ideas.

Travis was writing, too. Justin looked over at his paper. Travis wasn't working on their project. He was writing a note to someone.

Maybe we could go out sometime
You are beautiful, you know.

Justin rolled his eyes. A major project was due next week, and Travis was busy writing a love note to his girlfriend, Kyra.

"So, what do you want to do the project on?" Justin asked. Travis looked at him blankly.

"I don't know. That's what you are supposed to be good at," he said. He smiled over at Rachel and Jessica at the other side of the room. They giggled and turned back to their desks. Justin knew this was going to be hard. He went through his books while Travis doodled and wrote letters.

By the end of the class Justin told Travis that he had decided on a topic for the project—tropical rain forests. Travis wanted to know if it always rained there.

Is he kidding? thought Justin. Justin took a deep breath and closed his books. The bell rang and they got up to leave.

"So, are you going to do some work on the project this weekend for me to look at on Monday?" Travis asked.

Justin turned around and looked him in the eye. He wasn't as tall as Travis, but he had to make his point.

"Listen, I will do this project with you, but I am not doing all the work. You have a brain. If you want to get part of the mark, you're going to do part of the work," Justin told him. He waited, expecting Travis to push him into the desks behind him.

Travis stared at him. "Are you trying to tell me what to do?" he asked. He towered over Justin and stared at him.

"I'm trying to explain how a project with partners works. This outline is due Monday. We have to come up with something together," Justin answered.

"Yeah, I know. I'll call you later—if I have time" Travis said. "By the way, what's your last name again?"

"It's Andrews," said Justin. He wrote down his phone number for Travis. "We should go to the library after school to start on this," he said.

Just then Kyra popped her head in the class. Travis walked over and leaned against the door. Kyra smiled up at him as they talked. The whole time, Travis held the note he wrote during class.

Just give it to her and get it over with, Justin thought. *You see her every single second of every day. But hey, I guess she needs it in writing, too.*

Kyra was in grade eleven, like Travis. She had shiny, straight brown hair. She was always dressed up and never wore jeans. If she wore jeans her father, Mayor Jennings, would be embarrassed. He wanted his daughter to look good so he would look good.

Justin waited. He just wanted Travis to give her the note and then come back to talk about starting the project. He didn't like to leave things until the last minute. He had a feeling he would be doing the work of two people. Or at least one and a half.

Kyra smiled and said good-bye to Travis. She waved at Justin. Kyra was on the volleyball team with Justin's older sister, Emily.

"Say hi to Emily!" she called in.

Justin waved back.

Travis walked back over to Justin's desk and gathered up his books. "What were we talking about?" he asked.

"The project," Justin answered. *You meathead,* he added in his head.

"Oh yeah, let me know what you think we should do. I'll call you tonight. I really need to get a good mark on this, Justin. I can't be taking this class over again next year. Do you understand?" said Travis. It sounded like a warning.

Justin thought about Travis's group of large friends. He thought how bad his life could be if he made Travis look like an idiot. Justin took it as a warning.

Why is this guy so popular? he wondered. *And how in the world did he get a girl like Kyra Jennings? She is smart, pretty, funny, and really friendly. It must be nice to be one of the "in crowd."*

Justin noticed that Travis was still holding the note in his hand.

"Hey, you forgot to give Kyra the note," said Justin, pointing to the piece of paper. Travis put the note in his pocket and waved to Kyra as she left the classroom.

Apparently, the love note wasn't for Kyra after all.

chapter 3

jealous

Justin had English class after geography. He took his seat in class and pulled out his copy of *The Catcher in the Rye*. The students took turns reading a page out loud. At the end of every chapter they talked about the theme and the characters. It was Justin's favorite book.

He looked around the classroom, but Mrs. Wismer wasn't there yet. Mrs. Wismer was the youngest teacher at Bayview High. She was married and was about four months pregnant. Mrs. Wismer was always leaving in the middle of class to barf. Of course, she didn't actually tell them that. Justin knew that's what she was doing. When Justin's dad got remarried, his new wife, Mary, had a baby. Mary barfed for six months straight.

Justin could see Jessica by the windows, laughing with her friends. Jessica was in all of Justin's classes. She just wasn't in first period shop class—or *chop* class, as they sometimes called it. The year before, some kid lost half a finger using the skill saw. Chopped it right off.

Jessica was holding a small piece of paper. She was reading it over and over again. Her two best friends, Rachel and Amanda, read it, too.

"Hey, what's so interesting over there?" Justin asked. They folded up the paper quickly and stopped talking. All three of them looked at Justin with wide eyes.

"Oooh, a little note there, eh?" he asked. "Care to share?"

"It's nothing, Justin. For our eyes only," she said. They all laughed. Justin noticed that the paper was about the size of the one Travis had in his hand. And the ink was green. The same color pen that Travis was using. Jessica blushed and slid the paper into her pocket.

Justin felt sick. Travis gave the love letter to Jessica. The worst part about it was, it looked like she was excited. He didn't know if he should tell Jessica that Travis already had a girlfriend. If he did, Jessica might think that he was jealous. Even worse, Travis would pound him if he found out.

It's not enough that the guy has one girlfriend. Now he needs another one? Justin thought to himself. *What do they see in him?*

For the next hour, Justin couldn't stop thinking about that stupid note. He had a hard time keeping his mind on *The Catcher in the Rye*. Mrs. Wismer left three times to barf. Justin kept looking over at Jessica. She was beaming. He couldn't help worrying that this jerk was going to break her heart.

After class, Justin went to his locker and packed his backpack. John walked by with his jacket on, ready to go.

"Are you walking or taking the bus?" John asked. He was munching on some chips.

"Walking. I'm short on cash these days," he answered. "Are you coming?"

"Sure. I could use the exercise," John said, slapping his stomach.

Daniel jogged by a second later. "Hey, do you want a lift?" he offered as he passed them. Daniel was always moving quickly wherever he went. He was wearing a black jacket with a red dragon on the back. It matched his black sports pants.

"Thanks, but you move so fast you'll probably be home before we even get out the front doors. I think we're just going to take the long way home," John called over.

Daniel kept jogging out the doors. He held his hands out to his sides as if to say, "Don't say I didn't offer."

Down the hall, Jessica, Rachel, and Amanda were talking to Travis and a few other guys. Coach Martins was walking through the doors.

"Hey John, I still have a spot for you on the football team. Start now and I may be able to give you some play time on the field next September," he called back. "I want you to think about it." The doors closed behind him before John could give him an answer.

John smiled at the coach's offer. It seemed that he was the only guy in school who didn't want a spot on the football team.

"Johnny boy would rather play a silly game of chess than a man's game of football," Travis called over. He was standing in the hall, still talking to the girls.

"If you had the brains, Travis, you might be able to understand the game of chess. Those little kings and horses aren't just for playing around with, you know," John answered. He kept on walking and eating his chips.

The group started laughing. Justin turned around. He saw Jessica standing beside Travis. She was laughing and tossing her hair around. All of a sudden, Justin felt jealous.

All the way home Justin complained about Travis. He tried to only talk about how bad Travis was at geography. He didn't mention Jessica or the love note at all.

"Travis wouldn't give me the time of day outside of geography. Suddenly I'm his best pal in class, though" Justin said. John didn't say anything, he just gave Justin a look.

"What?" said Justin.

"Nothing," John answered, grinning. "I just think you might be mad for another reason. Maybe because Jessica was talking to Travis after school?" he joked. Justin punched him in the arm.

Soon they got to the corner of Main Street and Second Avenue. Justin turned left to go home. John kept on going down Main Street.

"See you tomorrow!" John said. "And don't worry. Guys like that don't win in the end."

"You are so wise," Justin joked. He wanted to believe John, but the truth was, he didn't. As far as Justin could tell, if you hung out with cool people, you had a cool life. Otherwise, you went home to do someone else's homework.

Justin walked up to his big, old two-storey house. He noticed that Mary's small blue car was in the driveway. There was a baby seat in the back. A yellow *BABY ON BOARD* sign dangled in the back window. That sign caused Justin a lot of grief when he was riding in the car. He was sure that people laughed at him.

Justin walked into the brick house and dropped his backpack in the corner. He took off his shoes, threw them into the closet, and hung his jacket on a hook by the door. The ledge above the hook had *Home Sweet Home* painted on it.

"Hi!" Justin called as he walked through the hall toward the family room. He heard squeals coming from the family room door.

"Hello, little man," Justin said. He bent down to see his baby brother swinging and jumping from the door frame. Baby Matthew was slipped into a little harness that hung from a long spring. The spring was attached to the top of the door frame. The spring squeaked when Matthew jumped. The tips of his toes touched the ground. When he kicked out like a frog, he sprang into the air. Whenever Matthew saw Justin, he jumped up and down and back and forth like a little wild man.

"Aaaah, pppplllt," Matthew spit. He gave Justin a raspberry right in the face. Spit sprayed everywhere.

"Good, you deserve that," Mary said as she came out of the family room. "Since you're the one who taught him how to give raspberries." She was laughing.

"How can that swing be fun, little man, huh?" Justin asked Matthew. "You must have one bad wedgie hanging from your butt like that." Matthew smiled and jumped.

"Justin! You're terrible!" Mary said. She smiled and went into the kitchen. "Do you need a snack? Dinner will be in a little while."

"No thanks, Mary. I'm just going to my room for a bit," he answered.

A few years ago, Mary had married their father. She suddenly found herself the stepmother of two almost-teenagers. She was very pretty, and wore her long, blonde hair in a clip. She was very good to Justin and Emily. They all had an understanding. Emily and Justin loved Mary as a friend, but she wasn't their mother.

Matthew, on the other hand, was different. Justin had not been happy at the thought of a new baby. Once he arrived, though, Emily and Justin were hooked. They both loved him to bits.

Justin heard a loud noise come from the direction of Matthew's jumper. He knew the sound well. It came from his diaper.

"Excuse you!" Justin said as he stood up. "And by the way, you stink." Matthew smiled and jumped.

Justin went up the stairs and into his room. He opened his backpack and spread some geography books on the floor. He did some work and then spent the rest of the night playing video games. He had the rest of the weekend to work on an outline for the project. He knew this project would be a good one. He was going to show how cutting down rain forests affected the wildlife and plants. He was even planning on including pictures from the Internet. It was going to be awesome.

Travis didn't call all weekend. By the time Justin went to bed on Sunday night, he had only one thing on his mind. How much he hated being partners with Travis.

He knew the project would get him good marks. Little did he know that it would also get him into the "in crowd."

And a whole lot of trouble.

chapter 4

public enemy #1

Justin woke up early on Monday. It wasn't as though he had a choice. Matthew started squealing in the kitchen at six o'clock in the morning. Mary was doing some laundry downstairs. As hard as he tried, he could not go back to sleep.

Emily was already downstairs feeding Matthew. Her long, shiny black hair was tied back in a tight ponytail. Justin thought Emily looked just like their mother. She had long, dark eyelashes. Emily looked more Asian than Justin. Their mother had been born in China.

He could almost see his mother standing there, laughing. Sometimes he felt like she was right there with him in the room. But that was impossible. His mom had died five years ago.

"Hey, I didn't see you much this weekend," Justin said.

"I had a dance competition and an essay due. If I wasn't at the studio, I was at the library," she answered. She smiled at Justin. "If you want to get a ride with me, you'd better go and have a shower. By the way, your hair looks hilarious," she added. Justin ran his hand through his hair. Every single morning, he had a bad case of bed head.

"Well, hurry up and have a shower!" she said to Justin. "My volleyball practice starts at seven, and I want to get there a bit early." Emily was already dressed in her gym clothes. She took a cloth and wiped Matthew's face. He had spit baby food all over his high chair. It was all over his face.

"And don't forget your lunch. It's in the fridge," Emily added.

Emily babied Justin, almost more than she babied Matthew. When their mother died, Emily was twelve and Justin was eleven. She stepped in to "look after" Justin. Now that he was sixteen, he didn't really need it anymore. Somehow, though, neither one of them could bear to give it up.

Justin took a quick shower and got dressed. Emily waited at the door, tapping her foot. She was never late for anything a day in her life. Justin grabbed his coat and his backpack and ran out the door. He didn't know why he hurried to get a ride. He was going to be two hours early for class. But he was awake anyway. And he liked driving in with Emily.

When they got to school, a lot of students were already there. Choir, volleyball, and field hockey were just getting started. Justin went to the library to read for a while. He was still trying to figure out how to get a new partner for geography. He had spent all weekend doing the outline for the project. Travis hadn't helped at all. He decided he would tell Travis exactly what he thought of him. He was going to tell Travis off for not helping with the outline.

Before he knew it an hour passed by. The halls were getting busy.

"Hi," a girl said as she put her books down on the table. It was Lisa Benneto.

Justin looked around the library. He didn't know why Lisa was suddenly sitting with him. There were plenty of empty tables. The gorgeous girls of grade eleven rarely talked to him.

"I heard you and Travis are doing a project together," she said. She opened her grade eleven math book and started to do some homework. "He says you're really smart."

Boy, word travels fast over a weekend, he thought. Justin was so annoyed thinking about Travis that he didn't even notice that Jessica was sitting by herself.

Justin was starting to sweat. Before he knew it, Jennifer McBride and Becky Robinson sat down, too. Justin looked at his book and pretended to read.

Travis came into the library and put his books down on the table.

"Hey man, so how's the project?" he asked. He smiled at the girls and offered everyone at the table a piece of gum.

"Uh, great. I already have it all worked out," he answered. He had planned on telling Travis off. Instead, he just sat there, fishing out a spare copy of the outline.

"Isn't he the best? He's probably the smartest guy in grade ten," Travis said to everyone at the table. He flashed his famous grin, complete with perfect teeth. Travis slapped Justin on the back.

"Wow Justin, that's really great. How are you at grade eleven math?" Becky asked. She smiled and closed her books. "I could really use a hand."

Justin nodded. "Sure Becky, anytime. Just let me know. I might be able to help a little bit."

Travis saw Jessica sitting across the room. He left the table and walked over to talk to her. Jessica chatted for a minute or two, and then she got up to leave. She was smiling. Justin wondered when she was going to find out that she wasn't the only girl Travis had his eye on.

She waved at Justin as she left the library. "See you next period," she called to Justin.

Travis looked at him funny. He walked over to him and asked, "Are you friends with her?"

"We're in the same class. Yeah, we're friends, I guess," Justin answered. Travis looked worried. They all packed up their books and moved out into the hallway to head to their first classes. Justin passed by John and Daniel in the hall. John was just getting his books out of his locker. He was almost always late.

Beside the library, Jamal Richards was talking with the girls. He was another one of Travis' friends. He was the biggest and tallest boy at Bayview. Jamal was massive. He could have posed for *Musclebound Magazine*. Under his picture it would say "no matter how hard you try, you will never ever look as good as him."

Jamal's hair was completely shaved off, and he had a small black patch of beard on his chin. His deep, booming voice could be heard down every hall. When Jamal made a hit in football, the ground shook and the entire school heard the crash.

Jamal struck fear in most people—except for John. John thought he had an "understanding" with Jamal. They had worked together on the yearbook the year before. Now John thought they were great friends.

John closed his locker. He and Daniel walked down the hall toward the library.

"Bro, wazzup?" John said as he passed Jamal. He held his hand up for a high five. "I heard what happened at the game last week. That's *whack!"* he added. He suddenly had a swagger to his walk. Lisa and Becky looked at John and shook their heads.

Jamal did not give John a high five.

"Why do you always talk to me like that?" Jamal asked. He looked annoyed. In fact, he always looked a little annoyed when John talked to him like that. "Who do you think you are? Chris Tucker?" The girls laughed.

John had no idea that he sounded foolish. He just kept on walking.

And then there was Daniel. In a land of giants, he really looked short. He didn't seem to care. Daniel Thorne was always in a good mood. Justin noticed that Daniel had his share of female visitors at his locker.

"Daniel, wait up!" called Kyra from her locker. Daniel stopped and waited for her to catch up. Then they walked to class together.

Travis stepped out of the boy's bathroom just as Daniel and Kyra were walking past the door. He looked mad.

"What is she doing hanging out with him?" Travis said, still zipping up his fly. Jamal looked down the hall and shrugged his shoulders.

"Kyra!" he called after them. Kyra looked back over her shoulder for a minute. Then she turned back to talking with Daniel.

"Hey, Kyra!" he called out again. She turned the corner and was out of sight.

"She probably didn't hear you," Jamal said. They all knew that was impossible. Kyra wasn't that far down the hall.

"I don't know. She has been ignoring me all weekend. And she didn't call me back last night," he said. He looked at Justin. "Did you say something to her? About the note?" he asked. He moved closer to Justin and frowned.

"I didn't say anything," Justin answered. Suddenly, a loud ring sounded in the hall. He was saved by the bell.

Justin went to "chop" class and then hurried off to drama class. He stopped when he saw Travis, Tom, and Dave standing near the fountain. They thought drama class was stupid. He took a different way to the drama room so they wouldn't see him.

The day was going fine for a Monday—until lunch period.

Justin and John headed for the cafeteria after drama class. As they walked toward the doors, Travis and Dave called Justin over.

"Justin, buddy," Travis said. "We have geography together next period, right? If Mr. Thomas calls on us, help me out. Try to make it look like I did at least some of the work, okay?" he grinned. "Come on, we can talk about it over lunch," he added. He stopped smiling when he saw John walking toward them.

"Oh great, the chess king. Will you be joining us for lunch, too?" Travis asked John. He was giving John a dirty look.

"No. Thanks for the offer, but I'd rather keep my lunch down. I'm not staying anyway," John said. He looked at Justin, but he was looking out the window. Justin pretended not to notice that John was there. He really wanted to eat lunch with Travis and the rest of the "in crowd."

John shook his head and walked away. Justin felt a little guilty watching John leave the school by himself. He knew he should have stuck up for his friend.

Just then, Kyra walked by with Daniel.

"Hey babe, where have you been?" Travis asked. He tried to walk over to her, but she pushed him away.

"I've been busy," she answered. Travis looked at Daniel and then back at Kyra.

"What's your problem?" he asked. He was glaring at Daniel now. Jamal and Tom joined the circle. Some people just inside the cafeteria door peeked into the hall. They wanted to see what was going on.

"I don't have a problem anymore," she answered. Her face was getting redder and redder. She was clenching her fists. "I heard about your little love notes, Travis. Very sweet. Tell me, how many of those do you hand out a week?" she said. She was starting to yell.

"I don't know what you're talking about," Travis answered. He looked embarrassed.

"You know what? You're a loser. A dumb, conceited loser. I don't want to go out with you anymore," she yelled.

"Kyra, come on." He looked around to see who was watching and reached for her arm. "Give me another chance. We can work this out," he said quietly.

"Well gee, Trav, I would like to, but I'm kind of seeing someone else right now," she answered. She smiled and walked into the cafeteria holding hands with Daniel.

Within minutes, Daniel Thorne went from nicest guy in grade eleven to public enemy number one.

chapter 5

hanging out

No one in the group ate their lunch. They stood in the hall listening to Travis go on and on about Daniel and Kyra.

"Daniel ratted on me. I know it!" said Travis angrily. "He knew about the note and thought he could steal my girlfriend," he said with his fists clenched.

"Let me get this straight. You wrote a note to some other girl, and your girlfriend found out. And now it's Daniel's fault?" Jamal said.

"You know those sensitive guys," Travis said. "Always talking to the girls, listening to their problems. They never make a move, but they somehow worm in as a girl's best friend. Before you know it—BAM! They're stealing your girlfriend."

"Gee, let me think. Sounds like your problem started when you wrote a love letter to another girl," Dave said. He and Jamal both started to laugh.

"What are you, a suck or something? Shut up. This is Daniel's fault and he's going to pay for it," he said. He glared at Dave. Dave didn't say anything else.

It was clear to Justin that Travis was the leader of the group. It made perfect sense. His house was always parent-free, he had great cars, money to spend, and girls always hung around him.

"Daniel is not a bad guy," Jamal said. "You have no proof that he even knew about the note."

Travis didn't listen.

After lunch, Justin and Travis walked to geography class. Justin was starving. He hadn't eaten anything for lunch.

Mr. Thomas was at the front of the class. "Welcome, gentlemen. You are late," Mr. Thomas said. Jessica smiled at them as they walked in. Justin noticed that Jessica looked especially nice that day. She was probably trying to impress Travis.

They sat down and opened their books. Travis grabbed a copy of the outline Justin worked on. He handed it to Mr. Thomas.

"Here you go. We worked on this all weekend," Travis said. He turned around and smiled at Justin.

"Very good, Travis. I'm glad to see that you are taking such an interest in the class," Mr. Thomas said. He was reading over the pages quickly. "Just a reminder to all of you that this project is due on Friday. Your mid-term exam is next Monday. I will have a look at your outlines tonight and make suggestions. Keep up the good work."

Travis grinned at Justin. "We rock," he whispered, and elbowed Justin in the arm.

No, I rock, Justin thought to himself.

"That exam is going to be a killer, huh?" Travis whispered again. He was doodling on his note book.

"I don't think so. If you just make some study notes from your class notes, you won't have a problem. Then all you have to do is review your notes," Justin whispered back.

Mr. Thomas stopped what he was doing at the front of the class and looked at Justin. "Do you mind?" he asked.

"Sorry," Justin mumbled.

Travis chuckled.

Travis didn't write down a single note during class. When geography was over, Justin tried to talk to him about meeting at the public library that night. Travis, however, had other plans. He left the room quickly to go find Kyra.

After school, Justin found Travis in the hall by the library. He was getting ready to leave with Tom and Jamal.

"Hey Justin, come over here a minute," Travis said. Justin went over to the doors by the library. His plan was to give Travis little parts of the project to do on his own. Then Justin could look over his work, make changes, and hand it in. That way, at least Travis would be doing part of the work.

They only had four nights to work on the project. Justin had a good outline. It would be plenty of time to write a good project.

"Hey, the guys and I were just talking about Wednesday night. We usually hang out at my place on Wednesdays. My parents have meetings every Wednesday," said Travis. "We're heading over to my place right after school. Do you want to come? You could bring those study notes you were talking about," Travis said. He smiled and patted Justin on the back.

"Well, I…" Justin started to answer. He had drama club on Wednesdays, and then he had to be home to watch Matthew. Justin didn't get the words out.

"Come on dude, we always order pizza and watch a DVD," Dave said. Justin was impressed. The "in crowd" wanted him to hang out with them. Suddenly he forgot all about drama club. And Matthew. He wasn't going to miss this for the world.

"Okay," said Justin. "Here," he said. He handed Travis a list. "It's a few things to research for the project." Travis stuffed it in his backpack. They decided they would meet on Thursday night to put their research together.

When Kyra walked by, she said "hi" to Justin and Jamal but ignored Travis.

"I'm out of here," said Travis. He ran up to her. Travis tried to talk to her, but she ignored him and kept walking. When she got to the end of the hall, she stopped.

He smiled and nodded at the guys. "See, she is waiting for me. I told you I would get her back," he called over to them.

He started to walk down the hall toward her. All of a sudden, Daniel popped out of the bathroom and walked up to Kyra. He put his arm around her shoulders, and they walked out the front doors together.

Travis was left standing in the middle of the hall. He turned around and went straight to his locker. He got out his football gear. Then he slammed his locker and stomped toward the change room.

Daniel was public enemy number one. Now, he was on Travis's hit list. And the first hit would happen soon.

chapter 6

the plan

Justin spent Monday and Tuesday night working on the project. By Wednesday morning he was almost done his part of the research. Justin had it all set up in his computer. He hoped Travis was doing his share of the work. Justin had given him a number of things to research. The project was depending on it. There were whole sections that were completely blank on the computer screen. *No problem,* he thought. *I have time to hang out at Travis's place tonight. Thursday night I'll just copy Travis's work into my computer file.*

On Wednesday morning, Justin woke up to someone slapping his face. Tiny little hands slapped him over and over again. Someone was giggling, too.

"That's good, Matthew! Now say wake up Justin!" Emily said. She was sitting on the edge of the bed holding onto Matthew. Matthew jumped up and down on the bed.

"Is that all you do? Jump?" Justin grumbled as he rolled over.

"Hey, it's seven-thirty, you know. You'd better get going. And don't forget that Mary and I are going to yoga class tonight. You said you'd watch Matthew," Emily reminded him.

Justin groaned. "You know what Em? I can't," he said.

"What do you mean you can't? You said you would!" Emily said. She picked up Matthew off the bed and started for the door.

"I have, uh, my project to work on, and I'm meeting with Travis tonight . We only have two more days left to finish everything," he lied. Justin knew they wouldn't be doing homework at all tonight.

"Can't he come here?" Emily asked. Justin would regret this.

"No, he can't. He has high speed Internet. We need to download a lot of stuff. It would take forever here," he answered.

Emily sighed and shook her head. "Fine then. I guess Mary can't go unless Dad comes home early. You know, Justin, you hardly have to do anything around here. When you say you will do something, you should keep your word," she said. She walked out of the room with Matthew. Matthew peeked over Emily's shoulder and gave Justin a raspberry.

Justin got dressed quickly and flew out the door. The air was still cool, but it was getting warmer every day. Most of the trees were starting to bud with leaves. He took a deep breath of the cool spring air. He put his hands in the pockets of his jeans to keep them warm.

Justin was late for shop class. He breezed in just in time to get a detention. Mr. Jones, the shop teacher, handed him a yellow slip.

DETENTION:
Justin Andrews, 3:30 – 4:00 p.m.

Justin would just have to skip it.

During drama, John ignored Justin. He sat with some other guys in class. Justin sat in the back corner. Mr. Thomas told everyone again that the drama club was meeting after school.

Now Justin would have to skip drama club and detention.

"Hey, are you excited?" Jessica asked. She sat down beside Justin.

"About what?" he answered.

"You know, drama club? Give me a break. You've been looking forward to this for a month!" she said.

"Oh. That," he answered. He didn't say anything about not going. He knew she would try to talk him out of it.

At the end of class Justin sprinted down the hall to meet the guys for lunch. He ate with them all week. John didn't even bother to ask him if they were eating together anymore.

Justin caught up to Travis and asked him about his part of the project.

"Oh, yeah, I'm almost done," Travis said. He started to laugh and turned to talk to Julie.

"Well, do you want to give it to me on computer disk tonight?" Justin said.

"Justin, I've been working on that project all week. Tonight is for fun. But don't forget to bring your study notes for the exam for me to look over later," Travis said. "Hey, we have a lot of food to eat, and there's a game to watch tonight. We won't have time to talk about our geography project."

Justin had never been asked to hang out with the guys. He wasn't sure what game they were supposed to be watching. He didn't care, either. He would just hang out, eat, and enjoy having a social life.

Justin told Mrs. Wismer that he had to go to the doctor, so he could leave a little early from English class. He knew he would get in big trouble for skipping detention and drama club. But he was going to hang out with the guys that night, no matter what.

He opened his locker quietly and got out his backpack and jacket. Then he crept down the hall and went out a side door.

Freedom.

Justin walked all the way to Travis's massive brick house and went up the stone steps. Ivy grew up the house, and there were two pinecone wreaths on the huge double doors. Justin felt nervous. He rang the doorbell. A loud sound like church bells came from inside the house.

Travis answered the door with a soda in his hand. "Come in," he said. "Welcome to my humble home."

Justin walked in and couldn't believe his eyes. A huge glass chandelier hung from the high ceiling. A wooden staircase curved up to the second floor. To the right was a study. A leather chair and a large desk sat in front of a stone fireplace. The walls were lined with books. The whole room smelled like pipe smoke. *There must be a million books in there*, Justin thought to himself as he looked around.

To the left of the entrance was a formal living room and dining room. The dining room table had enough chairs for fourteen people. Justin thought of his own dining room. It had a small dining room table, with four chairs and lots of baby toys. All of a sudden, Justin felt very out of place.

They walked through the front hall and went through a door leading to the downstairs. The other guys were already there.

Travis's basement was a dream come true! A gas fireplace at one end. A small kitchen at the other end, complete with a stocked fridge and shelves of junk food. Beside it were a pool table and a sitting area. It had a big leather couch and matching chairs. There was a big-screen TV with a DVD player, surround sound, and a video-game system.

Justin sat down on the cold, soft leather couch. He sank right in and got comfortable.

Jamal was playing a video game.

"Hey," Justin said, trying to sound cool.

"Hey," Jamal answered.

Good conversation so far, he thought. Travis handed him a can of root beer and sat down.

"Okay, guys. We need to talk about something here," Travis said. Jamal looked over his shoulder and finished his game. Tom and

Dave were playing pool. They came over to the sitting area and leaned on their pool cues.

"First of all, my parents are going away for two weeks starting Friday. So, party on Friday night!" he said.

"All right!" said Dave and Tom at the same time. Dave gave Justin a high-five. Justin had never been to a real party before. He couldn't believe he was being invited. The only parties he ever went to were with John and a few of the other guys. There were never any girls invited. There was rarely loud music. Usually, parents were home.

"Second, I need to come up with a plan to take care of Daniel," Travis said. Tom and Jamal gave each other a knowing look. "You know how I feel. If you stab me in the back, you pay for it. I say we find a way make Daniel hurt a little."

No one said a word. Justin didn't like the sound of this at all. He wasn't quite sure if he heard Travis right.

Finally Jamal spoke up. "Look, Travis, just let it go. What are we going to do? Corner him and give him a beating?" he asked.

"Not a bad idea," Travis answered. Justin started to sweat.

They weren't really going to beat a guy up, were they? he wondered.

Dave sighed. "Come on. He's not even a big guy. We can't have five guys take the boots to him," he said.

Justin looked around and realized he was one of the five guys. His heart was pounding. He had never actually been in a fight before. Justin certainly wasn't going to give someone a beating.

"No, this is stupid. If you want to fight him yourself, then that's your decision. Five on one is not a fair fight," Jamal said. "We're not a gang," he added.

Travis looked angry. He stared into his can of root beer. "Fine. I'll take care of him myself. The least you guys can do is help me make his life a little, say, difficult," he finished. "Well, are you guys my friends or what?" he asked.

Jamal, Tom, and Dave nodded their heads in agreement. They didn't look very happy about it, though. All eyes turned to Justin.

"Well?" Travis asked.

Justin looked from face to face. He didn't want to be the only one to wimp out. They might not invite him over anymore if he did. He was actually enjoying having a social life for a change. He figured he could just hang back most of the time. He didn't want to beat on anyone or get into trouble.

Justin nodded his head. He was now part of the group. It was what he always wanted. Things were really looking up.

And then it all went downhill.

chapter 7

party on

On Thursday, Justin knew it would happen. He would have to pay for his "crimes" the day before. In shop class, Mr. Jones was hard on him for skipping detention. He gave Justin two more detention slips. He would have to stay twice as long that day, and again on Friday.

Mr. Thomas was a different story. Justin bumped into him in the hallway before first class.

"What happened to you yesterday?" Mr. Thomas asked. He had a water bottle in one hand.

"I had things to do," Justin answered. He wouldn't look Mr. Thomas in the eye.

"Justin, I had to choose all the roles for the school play last night. Now you don't even have a part. I thought you were looking forward to being on the big stage. What were you thinking?" he asked. This play would be Bayview's biggest play ever. Mr. Thomas had told Justin that he thought he had real talent.

"What was I thinking? I was thinking maybe I would have some fun that didn't revolve around the school for a change," he snapped. "Besides, I don't even know if I want to be in that dumb club anyway." Justin couldn't believe what he was saying to his favorite teacher. He waited for Mr. Thomas to get mad.

Mr. Thomas calmly took a drink of his water and stared off down the hall.

"Ok, if this is how you feel. But don't change who you really are just to make somebody else happy," he said. He was watching Travis, Dave, and Tom come down the hall. Then he looked back at Justin. "My door is always open, you know that." He turned around and walked toward his office.

Justin had the same talk with Jessica. She wanted to know why he hadn't shown up for drama club. When he told her he was hanging out with the guys, she wasn't impressed. Justin was surprised. He thought that she would understand that he couldn't turn down that kind of invitation. Besides, if she liked Travis so much she would surely be impressed that Justin was hanging out with him.

At lunchtime, the guys asked Justin if he wanted to go with them to meet the girls at Lee's Restaurant. Would Justin like to go in a sports car with some older football players to meet some girls? The question was a no-brainer. They took Travis's sports car, and he bought lunch for everyone. They had a great time.

After lunch, Justin asked Travis if he had done the research for the project. Travis smiled.

"I have it on disk, as a matter of fact. I can't come over tonight to work on it. Why don't you just add my sections to the project? All you will have to do is print it. Then we can hand it in tomorrow, okay buddy?" he said.

"Sure, that should be fine," Justin answered. He was amazed that Travis was doing his share. He figured he had an easy night ahead. Put the information in, fix it up a bit, and then print. It didn't quite work out that way.

After a long detention, Justin went home. He ate dinner, and then played with Matthew for a few minutes. Justin then took the disk Travis gave him and sat down at his computer.

When he opened the file he almost fell off his chair. The page was practically empty. A few lines were written on each section. The heading "rain forest wildlife" had two lines written under it. "Destruction of the rain forests" had a few lines written for it. He scrolled down the page. It didn't get any better.

Justin put his head in his hands. He had to finish the project by himself. Fast. He sat on his bed to crack the books again.

At ten o'clock that night, Emily popped her head in Justin's room to see how he was doing. He told her what had happened. She offered to help. Emily sat down at the computer and surfed the web for information. She even helped him edit some of the stuff he wrote. They finally finished at three o'clock in the morning. Justin fell into bed.

The alarm went off minutes after he fell asleep. At least, that was how it felt. His eye sockets even felt sore.

Friday was a blur. He made it through the morning without falling asleep. Mr. Thomas seemed happy with the work that he had handed in. Travis acted stunned that there was hardly anything on his disk. He insisted there must have been a disk error.

"I had written a lot of information, dude. Honest!" he said and shrugged his shoulders. Justin didn't believe him, but it was too late. He could either tell Travis off and miss the party, or let it go. There was nothing he could do about the project now, anyway. He decided he deserved some fun. Justin was more serious about going to the party than he was about worrying about the project.

One more long detention, and it was finally Friday night.

Justin was tired from hardly sleeping the night before. He started to get his second wind when he went home to change for the party. He couldn't wait.

"You're going where?" asked Emily when Justin asked her for a ride to the party. "I'm not driving you anywhere so you can hang out with that creep!" She was angry that Justin even wanted to go to the party after what Travis pulled. Justin wanted to go for sure. Mary was going out shopping with Matthew and offered to give Justin a lift. He went outside and got in the car. The yellow *BABY ON BOARD* sign swayed in the back window.

When they arrived, Justin ran up to the door. The music thumped loudly from inside. A sign was taped to one of the double doors.

Come in, shut the door, and come downstairs!

He took off his shoes, hung up his coat, and went through the basement door. He was only halfway down the stairs when he saw Jessica,

Rachel, and Amanda. Justin had to smile. He knew there was no way Travis would have a party without girls. However, Kyra was nowhere to be seen.

"Justin, my man, how's it going?" Travis called over to him. He walked over and slapped Justin on the back. "Make yourself comfortable. I think you know everyone here."

Justin looked around. There weren't very many people at this party. Just Dave, Jamal, Tom, a few other guys from the football team and the three girls. Jessica waved from across the room.

"I didn't know Jessica was going to be here," Justin said.

"I thought I should maybe keep my options open, just in case Kyra doesn't take me back," Travis said, laughing.

Justin walked away. *He is totally leading her on*, he thought. *Figures. I can't get any girl, and he has a waiting list.*

A game of pool was going on at one end of the room. There was food everywhere. Chips, tortillas, pizza, chicken wings—anything you could think of. Justin wondered how Travis paid for all this food. He never asked anyone to bring anything. As a matter of fact, he laughed when Justin offered. He said he had it covered. Justin figured his parents left him money to use while they were gone.

Justin walked over to Jessica and her friends and sat down.

"Well, well, well, look what the cat dragged in," Jessica said. She had a red long-sleeved shirt on with a pair of jeans that sat low on her hips. Justin thought she looked even better than she did at school—and she looked great at school.

"Hey, I'm a regular around here," he answered. "What brings you here? As if I have to ask," he said. He rolled his eyes and reached over the table for a handful of chips.

"We were invited. Besides all our other party plans fell through," she answered.

Rachel laughed. "As if we had other plans!" said Rachel. Rachel's dark curls were pulled back with a claw-like thing. Justin noticed it right away. He could never figure out why girls used them. Emily had a few of them. They looked like instruments of torture.

"So this is how you spend your time now, avoiding us drama folk," Jessica joked. She winked at Justin and took a drink of her soda.

Justin smiled. He was at a cool party with cool people. It felt good. Until the problems started.

chapter 8

who puked?

It wasn't long before the house was jam-packed with kids. He waited for the bathroom downstairs for at least ten minutes. He could hear laughter coming from inside. He rolled his eyes and decided he'd better look for another bathroom.

He went upstairs. There were a few people hanging out in the kitchen.

He went up the winding stairs and found a bathroom at the end of the hall. This time, there weren't three giggling girls in there.

When Justin came down the stairs the kitchen was completely full of people. Even more were coming in the door. Everyone was yelling because the music was so loud.

"Justin, come over here for a minute," Tom called out. Justin walked into the kitchen. Tom was talking to a group of girls. He put his arm around Justin. "This is my buddy Justin. Justin, this is Amelia and Annie," he announced. Amelia and Annie looked like models. Tom was grinning from ear to ear.

"Nice to meet you," Justin said, smiling. He shook hands with the girls, and they talked for a minute. He couldn't believe how many good-looking girls there were at this party.

"Are you coming to the basketball game tomorrow? We're playing Lincoln High. Amelia here goes to Lincoln. She says she may go to the game, too," Tom said. He was now leaning against the wall, trying to look casual.

"Yeah, I think so," Justin answered. He was at a party, and now he was also going to the game tomorrow. And Amelia might be there. Life was so good.

Justin went back downstairs to play a game of pool with Jamal. The basement was packed with people. Some were dancing. Others were just hanging out and talking. Justin couldn't believe how many people were coming out to this party. Every ten minutes there were at least twenty more people.

The pool table finally opened up, and Jamal asked Justin if he wanted to play a game. Little did he know that Justin was the king of the pool table. Justin spent most of his time at John's house playing pool in his "toy room." The name, toy room, had stuck from when they were kids, but the toys had sure changed. The dinky cars and action figures were exchanged for a pool table and a TV. Justin was a pool expert. This was his chance to impress everyone.

Jamal, however, was a great player. They were pretty much tied up by the time the last few balls were on the table. A crowd had formed around the pool table. Justin was bent over to set up a shot. He had the seven and the five ball in line with the white ball. All he had to do was knock them in.

"Green and orange, corner pocket," Justin called. He pulled the cue back. Suddenly, he felt a poke in his sides. He jabbed the cue out, hitting the white ball hard. The ball bounced on the pool table and onto the floor. The crowd of people laughed. Justin almost died of embarrassment. He blew the game in front of everyone. Jamal took his final two shots and did a little dance to celebrate his win.

"Hey!" Justin called out. When he turned around, Jessica was laughing behind him.

"Just curious if you were ticklish," she said.

"Now you know," he said. His frown melted into a shy smile. How could he be mad at her?

He was just about to challenge Jessica to a game of pool when he heard a loud crash. It sounded like it was coming from upstairs. He ran up the stairs to see what happened. Five guys were standing on what used to be a coffee table. One of them was lying on the broken pieces of wood. He was barely able to get up.

It was only ten o'clock, and the house was packed with people. Justin hadn't even seen many of them before.

Some guys were emptying the fridge and the cupboards of food. Chips and drinks were spilt all over the floor of the kitchen.

Justin went back downstairs to warn Travis what was going on. Travis didn't seem to care. In fact, he looked like he was out of it.

"Dude. Dude!" Justin said. Travis leaned against the wall. "Hey, buddy, you need to know that there are way too many people in your house. They're going to destroy the place!"

"What are you talking about? I invited them all," Travis mumbled. His eyes were red, and he was slurring his words. He stretched his arms out wide. "They are all my friends. They love me," he added. He looked across the room. Two guys had put his mother's shoes on the pool table. They started shooting at them with their pool cues. Travis laughed and laughed.

"Are you nuts? Your parents are going to freak out! What is wrong with you?" Justin said. Two girls spilled a bottle of something red all over the carpet. Another girl, who was lying on the floor, rolled over it to wipe it up. The other girls giggled.

"Chill out. This is what we call fun," he said. He slid down the wall and sat on the floor.

Justin took a look around. It seemed like everyone was acting stupid. One girl was crying in the corner. Three guys were singing into a toilet plunger. The house was a total mess.

For the next few hours Justin went around cleaning up spills and stopping fights. Soon, he realized what was going on. The people who were acting like idiots were drinking.

When Justin walked into the bathroom, there was pee on the floor. He was not about to clean it up. He already spent most of the night stopping people from wrecking the place. He drew the line at cleaning up pee.

He almost tripped on Travis as he walked down the stairs. "Hey, what are you doing sitting here?" Justin asked. "Have you seen what a mess your house is?"

Travis didn't answer. Within seconds Justin knew why. At first the smell was faint. Then it got stronger. Justin covered his mouth and stepped back. Travis had puke all over himself. His perfect hair was matted and messy. His pants were undone, and his shirt was untucked.

Justin realized that maybe Travis was the one who had peed on the floor. Justin winced. He wondered if Travis had pee on his socks.

"Great party, huh?" Travis almost belched. "They love me."

Justin couldn't take it anymore. The people who were destroying the house weren't Travis's friends. They didn't even like him. As a matter of fact, some of them didn't even know him.

From the top of the stairs he could see people walking out of the house with stuff in their hands. They were stealing plants, CDs, and everything in between. Chairs were broken, the carpets were stained, and someone started signing the wall in red lipstick. It was a mess.

Justin looked down the stairs. Jamal was sitting on the bottom step. He walked down to see if Jamal was having the kind of "fun" that Travis was having. Jamal was fine. They both agreed that this party had to end, and soon. Justin knew that as uncool as it would be, someone had to stop this thing.

He picked up the phone and called the police. Then he called Emily.

chapter 9

close call

When Justin went downstairs on Saturday morning, Emily was lying on the couch watching TV. Justin walked in with his head down and sat on the floor.

"Good morning, party animal. How are you feeling today?" Emily said. She sat up and took a drink of her milk that was sitting on the table.

Justin smiled. "Tired," he answered. "Thanks for helping me clean up over there. And thanks for driving all those people home," he added. The police had got the kids out of Travis's house. But it was Emily who had helped put the pieces back together.

"Forget about that. What about Travis? It took you, me, and Jamal to move him to the bathtub and rinse him off. I bet he has never had a bath with his clothes on before," she said. They both laughed.

"What an idiot. He made a fool of himself and trashed his parent's house. Then he went to bed soaking wet. Serves him right," she added.

"I know," he said.

Justin thought about the long night. Jessica had gone around the house putting trash into garbage bags. Jamal, Emily and Justin cleaned up Travis as much as they could. Emily drove drunken people home. Some had to leave their cars at Chris's house. They might have otherwise driven and killed someone on the road. The whole party had been a total waste of an evening.

"Thanks for all your help. I'm really sorry. I just didn't know what to do. It was such a mess," he said quietly. Emily smiled.

"Look, I'm glad you called. I would rather come and help you than let you get into a bad situation. Just do me a favor. Stay away from house parties. They're never as much fun as they sound," she stated.

Justin spent the morning going over his study notes for the exam on Monday. He knew the stuff inside and out. He was going to get an "A" for sure. After lunch, he took a shower and decided to go to the basketball game.

By the time he showed up at school Saturday afternoon, the basketball game had already started. Travis and Dave waved Justin over. They had courtside seats and saved him a spot.

Justin sat down beside Travis. "You look a lot better today than you did last night," Justin said.

"Yeah, I know. I was a mess. Jamal said you and your sister helped clean up. I guess you guys also, you know, got me into bed," Travis said. He wouldn't look at Justin. "Thanks."

"No problem," Justin answered. "How is the mess coming along? We could only do a bit last night. It was such a disaster."

"Oh, I called a cleaning service. They'll probably be there all day," Travis said.

Must be nice to have the money to buy your way out of problems, Justin thought to himself.

Running shoes squeaked as the players ran up and down the court. Bayview High was already winning by 5 points. Justin noticed that Travis didn't watch the game at all. Instead, he scanned the crowd and watched the door.

Justin thought Travis was looking for Kyra. Soon, Justin realized who he was looking for.

Daniel was in the same row as they were. He wasn't too far down from them. Kyra wasn't with him, as far as Justin could see. Justin watched as Travis stood up and walked along

70

the bottom of the bleachers toward Daniel. He didn't even look at Daniel. He simply held his arm out to his side with his hand open. He slapped Daniel in the head as he walked by. Daniel didn't know what hit him. He looked around, but by the time he realized it was Travis, Travis was far away. Daniel ignored him and went back to watching the game.

The entire game went along like that. Travis threw things at Daniel, and once he walked by and stepped on his foot. Daniel wasn't doing anything about it.

He is probably too afraid to do anything, anyway, Justin thought. *I bet he has never been in a fight in his life, either.*

At half time, everyone went out into the crowded hallway. Travis bumped into Daniel on purpose. It sent him crashing into the lockers. Travis just kept on walking. Later, he followed Daniel to the water fountain. When Daniel bent over, Travis pushed his head down into the stream of water. Daniel got water up his nose, and hit his mouth on the metal spout. His lip split and blood dripped down his chin. Daniel stood at the fountain holding his face. Travis walked over to Justin and Jamal.

"Did you see that?" said Travis. Jamal wasn't laughing. Neither was Justin. "Come on, he's a big boy. I didn't do anything really bad," Travis chuckled. When he looked off down the hall his face fell. He wasn't smiling anymore.

Kyra was wiping Daniel's face. She saw Travis watching her. She gave Daniel a kiss on the cheek and then walked toward Travis. Without saying a word, she punched him in the stomach and then walked away. Travis doubled over in pain. Everyone in the hallway thought it was funny and started to laugh.

Travis was furious. He looked around for Daniel and Kyra, but they had left. "Come on," he said.

He stormed down the hall toward the front doors. Jamal, Justin, and Dave followed him. Justin was starting to regret coming to the game at all. He had a feeling that things were going to get very ugly.

"I'm going to take care of that weasel once and for all," Travis said as he marched down the hall to find Daniel.

Travis stopped and looked down the next hall. From the corner of his eye Justin saw Daniel and Kyra. They were over by the cafeteria. He could barely see Kyra, though. She was partly hidden behind the cafeteria door. He hoped Travis wouldn't notice them. Then maybe there wouldn't be a fight.

Seconds later, Travis saw them, too. Travis walked toward the cafeteria and rolled up his sleeves. Justin, Jamal, and Dave followed. Justin was worried. Travis grabbed Daniel by the shoulder. He swung him around, raised his arm, made a fist, and...

...stopped.

Mr. Thomas was standing in the cafeteria talking to Daniel. It had been impossible to see him from the hall.

"What is going on here?" Mr. Thomas demanded. His arms were crossed.

Travis let go of Daniel's shoulder and lowered his fist. Daniel didn't look scared at all.

"Nothing," Travis said. "I was just...oh, nothing," he mumbled. He turned around and went out the front doors. Travis got in his car and sped out of the parking lot.

chapter 10

the test

On Monday morning Justin was beat. He had spent all day Sunday studying for the geography exam. Mr. Thomas was known for his tough exams, but Justin felt ready. He walked into class and sat down at his desk beside Travis.

"Hey, what's up?" Travis asked. He was leaning back in his chair with his legs stretched out in front of him. His feet were crossed at the ankles. He threw a smile to Jessica.

"You look awfully happy," Justin said. "Are you prepared for this exam?"

"Sure. I'm sitting here, aren't I?" he asked. He smiled and got out a pen.

"Yeah, I guess you wouldn't be here if you hadn't studied," said Justin.

"No, I mean, I'm sitting HERE. I'll do great," Travis said. He punched Justin in the arm.

Mr. Thomas walked in with a stack of paper in his arms. He gave a bunch of exams to each person at the front of the class.

"Okay, you know the rules. Pass them back and place one on your desk, facing down. When I give you the word, you may turn your papers over and begin. No talking, no cheating, and no leaving the class before at least an hour is up. I want you all to try your best," he said.

The papers were passed down the rows. When everyone had an exam face down on their desk, Mr. Thomas said, "Begin."

Justin turned over his paper and began writing. Some of the questions needed one-word answers. Some needed long answers. The long essay questions were near the end of the exam.

The room was silent except for the scratching sound of pens on the desktops. After only twenty minutes, Dean Moore walked up to Mr. Thomas' desk. He handed in his paper. Everyone looked up.

Dean looked upset. Mr. Thomas whispered something to him. Dean had trouble in school, even though he was smart. Mrs. Wismer told him that some people just learn differently than others. He was allowed to take his English exams in the hall. That way, he could talk some of the questions over with Mrs. Wismer.

Dean followed Mr. Thomas out into the hall. He took his exam along. The door closed, and the class went back to their work. Mr. Thomas came back in, and then went out again a few times during the exam. Dean was out in the hall, sitting on the floor.

No one said a word when Mr. Thomas left the room. They knew if they were caught talking they would have their exams ripped up and tossed in the trash can.

Justin worked quietly on his exam. He answered the short questions quickly. Finally, he came to the essay question section.

I am going to ace this exam, he thought to himself. Justin felt strange – as though someone was staring at him. He looked over at Travis. Travis wasn't staring at Justin. He was staring at Justin's paper. When Travis saw Justin looking at him he looked back at his own paper. Justin moved his left arm across the desk to block his answers. When he glanced back at Travis, Travis gave him a dirty look. Later, Justin could have sworn he saw Travis looking at his paper again.

Justin finished his last question as Mr. Thomas walked to the front of the class. "Five more minutes," he said. Justin flipped through his pages to make sure he didn't miss anything on the test.

"Time is up!" Mr. Thomas called out again. "Please hand in your exams now. I will be marking them next period, so you should have them back tomorrow." Mr. Thomas always marked exams quickly.

Everyone got up and piled their exams on the teacher's desk.

Justin and Travis left the class and saw Dave and Tom standing at their lockers.

"How was it?" Tom asked.

"Not bad at all. Thanks to my man Justin here," Travis said. He smiled and slapped Justin on the back. Justin was surprised that Travis thought he did so well. He had only helped Travis with his homework a few times.

Travis made a fist and hit knuckles with Dave. They talked a bit about the upcoming football game. Then Justin ran went English class.

Mrs. Wismer was waiting for the class with a pop quiz on *The Catcher in the Rye*. Justin panicked. He hadn't finished the book. He had spent all his time studying for geography. He felt bad acing one exam and then not doing well on a quiz. He knew he should have studied more. But he was glad he had gone to a party and a basketball game this past weekend. He was finally having fun. His new friends were certainly keeping him busy.

After class, Justin walked to his locker. When he looked down the hall, he saw Travis talking to Mr. Thomas. They looked like they were arguing. Justin walked over right away. He figured his buddy had failed the exam. As he got closer he could hear Mr. Thomas talking.

"Someone in the class cheated on the exam," Justin heard Mr. Thomas say. Mr. Thomas must have thought it was Travis who cheated. Justin felt bad for Travis. Cheating was taken very seriously at Bayview High. If Travis cheated, he would be in big trouble. *The guy is drowning himself,* he thought.

Justin had no idea that he was the one who was drowning.

chapter 11

accused

Justin stood back from the conversation. He tried to think of a way to help bail out Travis.

"Then you tell me why your essay answers are the same," Mr. Thomas demanded.

"I told you, I don't know. I've been studying all year. Maybe Justin has been falling behind," Travis argued.

"Hey, what's going on?" Justin asked when he heard his name. He shifted his books under one arm. Mr. Thomas and Travis stopped talking for a minute and stared at him.

"Justin, I've been marking the exams from last period. Not only do you and Travis both have the same answers on the exam, but your essay answers are exactly alike. That is impossible. No two essay answers can be exactly the same, word for word. One of you must have cheated," Mr. Thomas said. He looked at both boys. He waited for Justin to answer him.

Justin looked from Mr. Thomas to Travis. Just what in the world was happening?

"Well, it wasn't me. I've been studying really hard this year." Travis insisted. "My parents will put me in military school if I get into any more trouble in school." He looked Justin square in the eye.

"Then that leaves you," Mr. Thomas said to Justin. "Did you cheat on the exam?"

Travis stared at Justin, and so did Mr. Thomas. Justin couldn't believe this. Now the guy was going to get him into trouble. After the project, the homework help, and everything. He didn't know what to do.

"One of you has to own up to it," Mr. Thomas said. "Or else both of you will be punished."

Justin didn't say a word. Travis shrugged his shoulders and put his hands in his pockets.

"I told you, it wasn't me. I saw him looking at my paper," Travis said.

Justin said nothing. *How could Mr. Thomas believe that I cheated?* Justin thought. *Great. If I tell on Travis, he'll get into big trouble at home and probably get me, too. But if I don't tell on him, I'll be the one getting into trouble.* He tossed both ideas around a bit. Justin tried to decide what to do.

"Is he telling the truth?" Mr. Thomas asked Justin. Justin wouldn't look at him.

"I guess so," Justin finally said. He stared at the ground, his heart pounding.

Mr. Thomas shook his head at Justin. He looked disappointed.

"Fine. Then you will get a failing grade on this exam, Justin. I want to talk to you for a minute. And you, Travis, may be excused," he said. He gave Justin one last look and walked into the classroom.

Travis smiled. He picked up his gym bag from the floor. "Thanks, man. I would've been dead," he said laughing.

Justin ignored him and went into the classroom to talk to Mr. Thomas. He was still in shock at what just happened.

Mr. Thomas was sitting with his feet up on the desk and his hands behind his head. He was looking at the ceiling, thinking.

"Come on in. Have a seat," he said. Justin put down his books and sat in a desk right across from Mr. Thomas. He was still staring at the ceiling.

"So. Now you're cheating off Travis. This is interesting," Mr. Thomas said. He kept looking up at the ceiling. "I have to throw out your test. How do you feel about all this?"

Justin shrugged his shoulders and shifted in his seat. "Bad, I guess," he answered. His stomach was in knots. He knew those exam questions well.

"I know what that whole scene in the hallway was all about. I know you know this material, Justin. Why are you covering for Travis?" Mr. Thomas asked. He put his feet back on the ground and leaned forward on his desk. "You don't need Travis to be cool, you know."

Justin rolled his eyes. "I'm not trying to be *cool*," he answered. He looked out the window to avoid Mr. Thomas.

"Whatever. All of a sudden you have a new group of older friends. Now you have a busy social life, and girls are around," he said. "You've dropped the drama club and your old friends. You're letting your marks suffer. It's not worth it, Justin."

"Yeah, I am having more fun. But I'm not trying to be cool or giving up my life. I finally *have* a life," he said. He started to stand up.

"You think about this for a while. Travis just accused you of cheating. This is a very serious problem, Justin. If I tell the principal that you cheated, you could be suspended or even fail the class. Is your new buddy worth that risk?" Mr. Thomas asked.

Justin grabbed his books and walked out the door. He tried to clear his head as he walked toward his locker. A few hours ago he was acing a geography exam. Now, he was being called a cheater. All of this because of a so-called friend.

He kicked half of a chocolate chip cookie that was lying on the ground. It smashed into the lockers.

That would be my head if I told Mr. Thomas what really happened, he thought. He opened his locker. His exam notes were lying on the bottom. He looked them over. The questions on the exam were the exact questions that he had written in his study notes. He couldn't help but laugh to himself.

There in pen and paper was the proof that he hadn't cheated. But Justin knew that he couldn't use it.

chapter 12

sent up the river

John walked up to Justin's locker. He had gummy worms in his hand. "Hey. What's up?" John asked. They weren't hanging out much anymore. Except for drama class, Justin hadn't seen much of John lately.

"Nothing. I've just been busy. What's up with you?" he asked. Justin felt a little uneasy. His new friends didn't really like John. They didn't invite John to parties or basketball games.

"Not too much. I saw what Travis did to you just now. About the exam," John said. He offered some gummy worms to Justin. Justin shook his head and turned back to his locker.

"You don't know what happened. It was just a mistake. No big deal." Justin said. He slammed his locker shut.

John wasn't buying it. "He sold you out! Sent you up the river. Soaked you. Hung you out to dry. Stabbed you in the back. Ratted on you. Dissed you…"

"Okay, I get it," Justin yelled. "Would you stop with your stupid sayings?"

"I'm just saying, how can you hang out with those guys when they crap on you all the time?" John asked. He reached into Justin's locker and took out the geography study notes. "Why didn't you show these to Mr. Thomas? He would have known you didn't cheat if he saw you had study notes like this," John questioned. He had a confused look on his face.

"Exactly. I wasn't going to hand the notes over in front of Travis and get myself beaten up," Justin shot back. He grabbed the study notes out of John's hand and shoved them back into the locker.

John looked down the hall toward the drama class. "Anyway, I'm walking home. Are you going that way or not?" he asked.

Justin put his backpack over his shoulder and looked down the hall. Tom, Jamal, and Travis were hanging out with Jessica, Rachel, and Amanda again. Travis called Justin over and jingled his car keys. Justin was angry. He wanted to talk to Travis about the cheating.

Maybe he would be able to talk to Jessica a little bit, too.

"Actually John, I have to get home right away to look after Matthew. I think I'll just grab a ride," he said. John shrugged his shoulders.

"Whatever," he said and marched down the hall by himself.

"Hey John, how are those wild chess parties going?" Travis called to John. John smiled and turned back to look at the group. They were all laughing and talking. Justin didn't say a word.

"Great. How is the lying, cheating, and stealing going?" John called back. Travis stopped laughing. John smiled and waved, and then he disappeared through the doors.

"He's next on my list," Travis growled.

"Hey, what happened back there with Mr. Thomas? I never looked at your exam once," Justin said to Travis as he walked toward him.

"Yeah, sorry about that, buddy. I got a little stuck a few times," he added.

"I'm going to bomb that class because of you," Justin answered. He threw his backpack on the ground. "I thought we were friends."

"Look, you and Mr. Thomas are buddies. He'll let you rewrite the exam and you'll ace it," said Travis. He leaned closer to Justin. "If I got blamed for cheating, my parents would send me to military school. I mean it," Travis whispered. He didn't want anyone else to hear him. "I needed some help, man. Life isn't so good these days. My parents think I'm an idiot and can't wait to get rid of me. You, you'll be fine. It's only one little exam. Like I said, he'll let you rewrite it anyway. I promise I won't do anything stupid like that again."

Justin was quiet for a minute. He hadn't thought about asking to rewrite the exam. Mr. Thomas had no real proof that he had cheated. He might let Justin write it again to prove himself. Justin felt a little better.

Travis put his backpack on the ground and went into the bathroom.

"Wait for me. I'll just be a second," he called.

Justin turned and walked over to Jessica. She had her hair in a ponytail and a script in her hand. She was holding a half-eaten ice cream bar in the other hand.

"Going to your practice?" he asked.

"Yes I am. Too bad you're missing out on this play. Of course, you're too cool now, aren't you?" she asked.

"What do you mean? You seem to hang out with these guys as much as I do. I enjoy hanging out with your *boyfriend*," he answered. He was talking quietly so the others wouldn't hear him.

"My boyfriend? Who are you talking about?" she asked. She looked around down the halls and back at Justin.

"Travis. The one you follow around all the time?" he answered.

Jessica started to laugh. "Travis? You think I like Travis? Boy, you are thick," she said. She shook her head. "That guy is a total loser."

"You don't think he is cool?" Justin asked.

"What's cool about a guy who will have nothing but a list of enemies when he graduates? He has bad grades, a bad temper, and a bad personality. What is there to like?" Jessica asked.

Justin was shocked. He didn't realize that other people saw Travis like that, too. He wondered how many other people saw right through him. He was even more shocked to find out that Jessica didn't like Travis after all.

"But what about when Kyra found out about the note and Travis started trying to get her back? Weren't you heartbroken?" he said.

"Who do you think told her?" Jessica answered. "Justin, I don't want some guy just because his family has money and he is cute. I happen to have high standards. Girls are not shallow, you know. Kyra deserved to know that her boyfriend was cheating on her. She also knew I didn't want him for myself," Jessica added.

"I just thought you liked him. You girls are always hanging around and talking with those guys," Justin added.

"So what? We like to have fun," Jessica laughed. "Besides, Rachel likes Jamal," she said.

Just then, Travis walked out of the bathroom. He called to the guys that it was time to leave.

All the way home, Travis explained his latest plan to finally take care of Daniel. He needed their help to do it.

The plan was simple—Travis would tell Daniel to meet him behind the the Pizza Pit next Monday night. There was nothing but an empty field behind the Pizza Pit. The music inside was always loud. He figured no one would see him or hear him. He needed the guys to be his "look-outs." Travis had one week to prepare.

Justin didn't like the plan at all. Being part of the "in crowd" wasn't so great.

Travis worked all week on his plan to beat up Daniel. He spent every lunch hour talking about getting back at him. By the end of the week, Justin was tired of all the talk about fighting. He didn't need any more trouble. To top things off, Travis only called Justin when he needed help with his homework. Justin was starting to feel like he was only around as a private teacher.

Being friends with Travis wasn't as fun as he had thought it would be. And now he was getting into trouble at school. Being accused of cheating on an exam was as bad as it could get, he figured.

Until the police showed up.

chapter 13

busted!

On Sunday afternoon, the phone rang. It was Travis. Justin was surprised. Travis never called him at home. They usually made plans at school.

"Hey listen, buddy, I need a favor," said Travis. He sounded really happy.

"Sure," Justin said. "What do you need?" He was ready for this. Justin was sure that Travis was only calling him for help with his homework again.

"Listen, my uncle is away. He asked me to move his boat out of the marina to get some work done. I have the trailer. Could you give me a hand?" he asked.

Of all of his big, strong friends, he was asking Justin. And this time, it had nothing to do with a project or an exam.

"No problem," Justin answered. "When are you going down to the marina?" Justin asked.

"Well, I'd like to go down there tonight. But I can't use my dad's car. You have a trailer hitch, right?" he asked.

"Uh, yeah, there is a hitch on my stepmom's car," Justin answered. "Why don't we go earlier, while it's light outside?" he added.

"Don't worry, there is plenty of light around the docks. It won't be a problem. I've moved his boat a thousand times," he added.

"Whatever. We can do it tonight then. But where are we taking it?" Justin asked. There wasn't much room on Travis's driveway for a boat *and* all the cars.

"Just over to my uncle's place," Travis answered. "It won't be far."

They decided that Justin would pick up Travis at seven o'clock that night.

Justin was worried that he would have some trouble getting the car. Emily had told Mary all about Travis. Mary and his father were asking Justin a lot of questions lately. He knew they didn't trust Travis. He decided to say that he was going over to John's place. They would let him borrow the car to go over there for sure.

Mary was so glad that Justin was going to spend time with his "good" friend that she didn't even ask any questions. She handed over the keys, and Justin left to pick up Travis.

It was getting dark when they pulled up to the marina. Usually, people didn't put their boats in the water until May or June. The weather was so warm that April, that most of the boats were already in the water.

They turned down the gravel road that led to the marina. The streetlights were already on when they got there. The marina clubhouse was dark and locked up. Justin was surprised that so many boats were in the water in mid-April. The trailer rattled as the car made its way down the road. Travis kept looking over his shoulder at the dark road behind them. He seemed distracted. Justin thought he was embarrassed about driving in his car.

"What's wrong? You don't like this car or something? It's not the car rattling, you know. It's the trailer," Justin said as he looked over at Travis.

"I know. Your car is fine. I'm just looking around. That's all," Travis answered.

Justin drove the car down to the water. Then he backed the trailer down a cement ramp that sloped into the water.

"I'll go untie the boat and drive it over to this ramp. Then we can push it up onto the trailer," said Travis.

Justin backed farther down the ramp. The trailer was covered in water. Travis went over to a small, white boat, started the motor, and drove it slowly toward the ramp. Then he cut the engine and drifted in closer to shore. When the boat was close to the trailer he jumped out onto the dock.

"Okay, now roll up your pants. We need to get into the water to guide the boat onto the trailer. Then we can pull it out," Travis said.

It sounded easy enough. Justin rolled up his pants, put on the rubber boots Travis brought along, and started walking into the cold water.

He heard a car rumbling down the gravel road. Headlights cut through the night and shone on Justin in the water. He covered his eyes from the glare of the lights and waded into the water. The car pulled up beside Justin's car.

"What are you doing there, son?" a man's voice said as he stepped out of his car. Justin looked over at him. It was a police officer.

"Hi," he answered. "Just helping my buddy move his uncle's boat." The headlights were still on, and the light shimmered off the water.

"What buddy?" the officer asked. Justin looked around. Travis was nowhere to be seen.

"Uh, I don't know," he answered. "He was just here."

"Could you please tie that boat to the dock and step out of the water?" the officer said gruffly. Justin found a rope attached to the side of the boat and tied it to the dock. The lights were on his face the whole time. He walked out of the water.

"Really, I wasn't doing anything. This is my friend's uncle's boat. I'm just helping him move it out of the marina," he said. He wasn't worried. Travis was probably back over at the dock, getting something he left behind. He would be back in a second to clear things up.

The officer asked Justin to put his hands on the car. Justin started to feel nervous. He did as he was told.

The police officer shined his flashlight over the boat. Then he walked up on the dock and checked the inside of the boat.

"How come you don't have the keys for this boat if it belongs to your friend's uncle?" he asked. Justin didn't know what to say. He didn't know why Travis wouldn't leave the keys in the boat. He looked over his shoulder to see if Travis was coming yet. "What is the boat owner's name?" the officer asked.

"I don't know," Justin answered. He was starting to sweat. He wasn't doing anything wrong, but all of a sudden he felt like a criminal.

The officer walked back over to Justin and frisked his pockets for weapons. He told Justin he could take his hands off the car.

"Son, are you stealing this boat?" the officer asked him. He looked Justin in the eye.

"No! I swear. My friend asked me to help him move it. It's his uncle's," Justin said again. It was the truth, but even Justin was starting to doubt the story.

"Is this your car?" he asked.

"It's my stepmom's car," he answered.

"Okay, can you please sit in the police car? We need to radio in to the dispatcher," he said.

"Sure. No problem, officer," Justin answered. He got into the passenger side and sat with his hands in his lap. He looked out at the dark lake and the docks. There was no sign of Travis anywhere.

The officer got back into the police car. He turned the computer screen toward him and punched in Mary's license plate number. He could tell that it wasn't a stolen car. He asked Justin for his driver's license and checked out those numbers on his computer, too. He sat back in his seat and studied Justin's face. Justin didn't say anything.

"Do you know what the penalty is for stealing?" he asked.

Justin shook his head and narrowed his eyes. "No, no, I told you, I wasn't stealing this boat," Justin said.

"If that's true, then I'm going to need to find your friend and his uncle," he said.

Just then another set of headlights came down the narrow road. Justin figured it was Travis coming back.

Maybe he went to get help when he saw the police coming. Maybe he found his uncle to come and stick up for us, he thought.

The car pulled up, and a man got out.

He walked up to the police car and leaned down to look in the window. It was Mr. Thomas.

"Excuse me, officer, but can you tell me what is going on?" Mr. Thomas asked. Justin figured Travis must have called Mr. Thomas for help. He felt a little better all of a sudden.

"What is your interest in this issue? Are you this boy's father?" the officer asked.

"No, *that* is my boat," he answered.

Justin gulped hard. He was in trouble. Big, big trouble.

chapter 14

caught red-handed

The officer got out of the car. Justin jumped out, too. The three of them stood in front of the police car, lit up by the headlights.

"This boy here says he was helping his friend move his uncle's boat," the officer said. "Is this true?"

Mr. Thomas looked at Justin. "Travis?" he asked. Justin nodded his head. Mr. Thomas looked out over the water and then up at the moon. He took a deep breath and turned back to the officer.

"Yeah, that's right. Justin and the other boy were moving the boat for me." Mr. Thomas said. "I saw the police car from my window. I live up on the hill. I thought I'd come down to make sure everything was all right," he answered. He handed over the ownership papers for the boat. The police officer checked to see if the registration number matched those numbers on the boat. Of course, it did. The officer gave the papers back to Mr. Thomas.

"Sorry about that, kid. We've actually had a few boats stolen from this marina. We check this marina out carefully every night," the officer said to Justin. "You should think twice about moving a boat at night. Next time, come during the daytime when the marina is open. Then you won't have any problems," he added.

"Don't worry, officer, there won't be a next time," Mr. Thomas said. The officer got back into his car and drove off. Mr. Thomas and Justin were left standing in the darkness.

"Well, can you give me a hand putting the boat back?" Mr. Thomas asked. Justin's heart was pounding. He was shocked. Justin almost helped steal his boat, and all Mr. Thomas had to say was "give me hand?"

Justin followed Mr. Thomas to the boat and helped him push it back into the water. Mr. Thomas jumped in, grabbed the keys from his pocket, and started the engine. He drove it a few feet away and docked it. Then he walked back to where Justin was standing.

"So, I guess you like my boat," he said.

"Honestly, I wasn't trying to steal it. I didn't even know it was yours," Justin said. He started to shiver.

"It's okay, I believe you," said Mr. Thomas. "We can't really do anything about Travis. He isn't here, but you are. I think you'd better do some thinking, Justin. Is this the social life you were looking for? Because getting put in jail for five to ten years doesn't sound like fun to me," he said.

Justin rubbed his forehead and tried not to cry. He had to bite his lip hard.

"Besides, you look a little odd with your pants rolled up and rubber boots on," Mr. Thomas added. He put a hand on Justin's shoulder. "Are you going to get home all right?"

That's it? I come out here at night and get caught trying to steal his boat and he asks me if I'll get home all right? Justin thought. *This is unreal.*

"Well, I need to get going. I still have papers to mark tonight," Mr. Thomas said. "Come by my classroom this week so we can talk, okay?" He got into his car and turned on the motor. Mr. Thomas waited for Justin to get into his car and pull out before he drove off.

Justin rumbled up the gravel road, pulling the trailer. He couldn't believe what had just happened. He drove straight to Travis's house.

He wanted to smash the trailer into the garage. Or the entire house. Maybe he could back it right up in front of the massive doors and the pinecone wreaths. Maybe back it into the beloved sports cars in the driveway.

He knew those were bad ideas. The last thing he needed was another visit from the police.

Justin couldn't stop thinking about his conversation with Travis. He also wondered how someone could be so rotten as to try to steal their teacher's boat. *How could Travis be such a jerk? How could I be so stupid?* he thought.

Justin tried to convince himself that his friend couldn't possibly be so bad. *Maybe he wasn't lying*, he thought. *Maybe they were supposed to get his uncle's boat out, but got the wrong boat by mistake. Maybe he panicked when he saw the police coming and ran. Maybe it was all just a big huge mistake.*

Justin felt a bit better by the time he pulled into the driveway in front of Travis's massive brick house. *Of course Travis wouldn't need to steal a boat*, he figured. *After all, he is filthy rich.*

Justin got out of the car and a light came on by the front door. Travis stepped outside with Dave and Jamal.

"Dude!" he called out. "You got away from the police?" He was laughing. Suddenly Justin realized that the whole evening hadn't been a mistake after all.

Justin marched up the driveway, up the front steps, and right into Travis. He shoved Travis out of his way and went into the house. Standing in the front hall, Justin turned around and saw the shocked faces of Travis, Dave, and Jamal looking at him.

"Tell me you didn't just mess with me and get me to drive down to the marina to steal a boat for you! Tell me you didn't totally sell me out and plan to let me go to jail!" Justin shouted. Travis actually looked a little scared. "Tell me the little rich boy wasn't going to steal a boat just for the fun of it. Huh? Can you tell me that?" Justin yelled. He couldn't believe how mad he was. This time, Justin wasn't afraid of a fight.

"Hey, don't come in here and shove me around, you cry baby!" Travis shouted back.

"Cry baby? Guess whose boat it was, you idiot? Can you guess? It belonged to Mr. Thomas. The only reason I'm not in jail right now is because he got me off the hook!" Justin shot back.

"Did you really trick him into stealing a boat, Armstrong?" Jamal asked Travis. He had his arms crossed and feet spread apart standing by the door.

Travis looked at Dave and Jamal. They were not smiling. Jamal walked over and stood beside Justin.

Travis cooled down a bit. His face broke out into a grin. "It was a joke, Justin. I wasn't really going to have you pull the boat out of the water. Besides, that small car probably couldn't have pulled it," Travis said.

Jamal shook his head. "I can't believe this," he said.

"Seriously!" Travis said. He laughed a little and held his hands out by his sides. "It was just a dumb joke. I don't go around stealing boats. You just seemed so serious lately, I thought you needed a laugh." He stuck out his hand for a handshake. "It was a bad joke, okay? I'm sorry."

Justin didn't shake his hand. He walked out the door, unhitched Travis's trailer, and got in the car. When he got home, he threw up.

chapter 15

help from a friend

Justin got up early on Monday morning and went to see Mr. Thomas.

"Good morning. I'm impressed. I was hoping you would come to see me. I had a feeling you might avoid me instead," Mr. Thomas said. He put down his newspaper and sat up straight in his chair. "So, what happened last night? Did you go straight home?"

"No. I went to see Travis. He says it was all a joke. He wasn't really going to take the boat," Justin said.

"Oh," Mr. Thomas said. "That was a pretty bad joke. I guess it would have been a *really* bad joke if I didn't show up to talk to the police."

"Yeah, well, that is what he said," Justin answered. He leaned back in his chair.

"Do you believe him?" Mr. Thomas asked.

The room was silent except for the clock ticking on the wall.

"I don't know," Justin answered.

"I think you do. But you have to make these decisions on your own. Who you choose to hang around with and what you choose to do for fun can affect your whole life," Mr. Thomas said. "I'm not going to give you a lecture. You're a smart kid. Just don't wreck your life to keep up with the cool crowd."

He leaned back in his chair with his hands behind his head.

"This may come as a shock to you, but I was not in the cool crowd when I was in high school," Mr. Thomas said. He was smiling when he said it. Somehow, Justin figured as much.

"I could have been, don't get me wrong. I know I look like a hippy to you, but I had fun in my day. And it wasn't very long ago, thank you very much," he said. "Some of the people in the cool crowd are great. They have their heads on straight and have a great future ahead of them. But some are going nowhere. Don't let them bring you down. In a few years, it won't matter who went to the "in" parties and who was in the chess club. What will matter is that you have made a good life for yourself," he added.

"I know," Justin answered.

"See that? I gave you a lecture after all. I love being a teacher," Mr. Thomas said, smiling. "By the way, about your exam. Someone gave me this." He held up Justin's geography exam study notes. "Your answers are on these study notes almost exactly the way you wrote them on the actual exam. I can make only one conclusion—you did not cheat. Therefore, you do not fail the exam."

Justin was relieved. He smiled at Mr. Thomas. Justin knew who gave the study notes to Mr. Thomas. It must have been John who helped him out.

"What about Travis, then?" Justin asked.

"Ah, yes. Well we don't want him taking this out on you, or the person who gave me these notes, do we? Therefore, his exam will be rewritten. No fault," he said.

Justin smiled and shook his head. "Why do you keep saving my bacon?" he asked.

"I don't know. Maybe I'm just repaying a favor that someone did for me a long time ago," he said. "Remember, it's all about choices."

Justin got up and shook Mr. Thomas's hand. "Thanks," he said. "For everything."

Justin went to his first class feeling much better. When he saw Travis during lunch period, he went the other way. He sat by his locker and ate his lunch alone. It felt good to hang out alone for a change.

"Hey, what are you doing eating in the hall?" Jamal asked as he walked out of the boys bathroom. He walked toward Justin's locker holding a plastic bag in his hand.

"I'm just thinking," Justin answered. "I don't feel like listening to Travis anymore." Justin knew he was pretty much going to be out of the "in crowd." He didn't really care anymore about looking cool.

Jamal sat down on the ground and leaned up against the lockers. "Yeah, I know what you mean," he said. He took four ham sandwiches, a juice box, an apple, and an orange out of his bag. He also had a small bag with six chocolate chip cookies in it.

"What?" he said when he noticed Justin staring at his lunch. "My mom makes it for me."

"Nothing. It just looks funny for such a big guy like you to have a little bag of cookies and a juice box, that's all," Justin answered. He opened up his lunch bag and pulled out a peanut butter and jam sandwich and a bag of little orange crackers shaped like fish. "I guess I shouldn't talk, right?" Justin said, laughing at his own lunch.

Jamal laughed and stretched out his tree trunk legs. They blocked half of the hall. He leaned back and took a bite of his sandwich.

"Are you going to the Pizza Pit tonight?" Jamal asked.

"No. I think I'll stay home for a change," he answered.

"I know. I don't really want to be around when Daniel gets beaten either," Jamal answered.

Justin had totally forgotten about Travis's plan. He couldn't let Daniel show up and get pummeled by Travis. He had to tell Daniel. But first, he had to come up with a plan of his own.

chapter 16

watch your back

In between classes, Justin searched the halls looking for Daniel. He didn't see Daniel all day. When he finished last period, he quickly ran to Daniel's locker. Daniel was there. He was just closing his locker as Justin hurried over.

"Hi, Daniel," Justin said quietly, looking over his shoulder. "Listen, I only have a minute. There is something you need to know," he said. Daniel frowned. "What are you talking about? Aren't you Travis's friend?" he asked.

"Actually, I'm John Case's friend. Anyway, has Travis talked to you yet today?" Justin asked. The halls were starting to fill up after classes. He knew Travis could walk by any minute. Justin didn't want to become number three on his list.

"No. We don't really hang out much, in case you haven't noticed," Daniel answered. He stared to sling his bag over his shoulder.

"Wait a minute. I'm trying to warn you. Travis is going to tell you to meet him at the Pizza Pit to talk things over. Don't go," Justin said to him.

"Why not? Maybe we should discuss a few things," Daniel said.

"He doesn't want to talk to you. He wants to get you there so he can start a fight. He says he is going to teach you a lesson for stealing Kyra," Justin whispered.

Travis was coming down the hall. Justin looked over and backed away from Daniel.

"Is that right?" Daniel asked. "Thanks for telling me. I appreciate it. I'll handle it from here," Daniel answered.

For some reason, he was smiling. Justin wondered how he could find this stuff funny. He was about to be beaten to a pulp.

Just then, Travis walked up. "What are you two talking about?" he asked and glared at Justin.

"Justin here was just telling me that I should stay away from Kyra," Daniel said. He was covering for Justin. Justin didn't say anything.

"Oh. Well, don't worry about that anymore. Actually, I feel bad about how I've been acting. I was wondering if you would like to meet at the Pizza Pit tonight—to talk things over," Travis said. You would never have known that he was planning an attack.

Looks can be deceiving, Justin thought.

"You know what? I think that's a great idea, Travis. Thanks for asking. I'll be there. What time?" Daniel answered.

"How about eight tonight?" Travis asked.

Justin knew the time already. It was had been chosen carefully. By eight o'clock, the dinner crowd would be gone. It would also be dark outside.

"Sounds great," Daniel said. "I'll see you there." He walked down the hall like a guy who just got great news.

Travis rubbed his hands together and laughed. He couldn't wait to meet Daniel later that night.

Justin was worried. As far as he knew, this could turn into an all-out slaughter. Jamal and Justin had agreed on a plan—they would show up and fight, if they had to, but they wouldn't fight on Travis's side. It was time someone stood up for Daniel.

Justin didn't say a word during dinner. He ate quickly and sat in his room until it was time to leave. He told Emily what was going on.

There was no sense lying anymore. He had already done enough of that.

Emily told him not to go. She finally agreed not to tell on him, if she could come along. Emily would wait in the parking lot in case of an emergency.

At seven-thirty they arrived at Pizza Pit. Justin went inside the dim restaurant and sat in a booth by the window. The red leather on the seats was ripped. The music was loud, and the place was filled with smoke.

Travis, Jamal, and Dave came in minutes later. Tom was the last to arrive. They all sat down at Justin's table and waited.

Justin looked out the window, wondering if Daniel would really show up. He thought that maybe Daniel would bring some friends of his own. Justin hoped this wouldn't turn out to be a gang fight. Then again, it wasn't impossible. Life was out of control these days. Besides, they weren't in the best area of town. Everyone knew that actual gangs had been hanging out in that area lately.

At eight o'clock sharp, Daniel walked in. Alone. Travis smiled and waved him over.

"Hi, Danny boy. I wasn't sure if you were going to show up," Travis said. He was putting on a good show.

"I wouldn't miss it," Daniel answered. "So, what did you want to talk about?" he asked. He looked at Justin and slowly nodded his head. Justin didn't know what it meant. Obviously, Daniel had a plan of his own.

"You know, it is kind of noisy in here," Travis said. "Maybe we could go outside and talk for a minute. Then I'm buying the pizza. What do you say?"

"Great idea," Daniel answered. Travis got up from the table and walked toward the back doors. He motioned to the rest of them to follow. Justin could tell that Travis was happy. Everything was going according to his plan.

They pushed the back door open and walked out into the dark, cool night. The field was completely black behind the Pizza Pit. The door closed behind them. Only one light lit up the back area. A big trash bin sat at the edge of the pavement near the grass. An owl hooted. It was a creepy scene.

Justin looked around. He expected to see a group of guys come around the corner and take their place beside Daniel.

No one showed up. Daniel was planning on fighting them alone.

chapter 17

flying fists

Justin looked at Jamal and nodded. He was glad Jamal had decided to show up and bring Dave, too. They had agreed to stand by and pretend to go along with Travis. But they were not going to let Daniel take a beating. They had a plan. If things got out of control, they would step in and help Daniel. Even if it meant an all-out fight. They were tired of getting into trouble because of Travis. This time, he was going way too far.

It was finally time to do the right thing. Letting Daniel face Travis alone, or worse, ganging up on Daniel, would have been wrong.

Justin was glad he had made the decision. However, he wondered how his nose would look after Travis broke it.

The single light flickered in the darkness. They could hear the loud music coming from inside. Justin was sweating, even though it was cold outside. He had left his jacket at the table.

What if Daniel has a weapon? Maybe that's why he's not worried, Justin thought. The possibilities got worse and worse.

"So," Daniel asked. "What did you want to talk about?"

Travis smiled and took off his jacket. "You know, Daniel, I never did like you. And then you stole my girlfriend. What were you thinking, short man?" he asked.

Daniel's face went serious. "Travis, I thought we were going to talk this out," he said. Travis raised his fists in front of him.

"Yeah, talk," Travis laughed. "I talk the best with my fists. How do you feel now? You've been marching around the school with my girlfriend and acting like you're better than me. You're nothing but a wimpy little geek. Your luck just ran out." Travis looked angry. He stepped toward Daniel and pushed his shoulder.

"Come on, you baby. Are you afraid to fight like a man?" Travis said. He moved forward again and bumped into Daniel.

"Oh, is this what you call man to man? What are you going to do, have your buddies here gang up on me? Come on. We aren't little kids. Fighting won't help anything," Daniel answered. He was letting Travis push him around a bit.

Justin clenched his fists. It looked like Daniel was going to stand there and take it. He had to be ready to help out.

Travis wiped his forehead with his sleeve and moved around like a boxer. He held his fists up, ready to connect with Daniel's face.

"Look, I just want you to know that I don't want to fight you. But if I have to defend myself, I will," Daniel said.

Travis laughed. "Oooh, I'm scared," he said. Travis moved toward Daniel and punched his arm. He was starting to get really worked up.

"Come on, Daniel, let's see what you've got," Travis said.

Justin and Jamal moved to stand beside Travis. They were prepared to hold Travis back. They didn't notice the small group that gathered in the shadows.

With one final grunt Travis swung a right hook. Justin winced.

Suddenly, Daniel's right arm flew up. He blocked the punch with his hand. His feet were planted shoulder-width apart. His knees were bent a little bit. His right hand was raised in the air and he threw Travis's fist back. Travis stumbled, but Daniel didn't move. His hands were still ready to block—or hit.

Travis lunged forward for another attack. Daniel bent down and flipped Travis over his shoulder. Travis landed with a thud on the pavement. He laid there moaning for a minute.

Daniel smiled at Justin. "I told you I could handle it," he said. "Ten years of karate finally paid off," he added. Daniel offered Travis a hand to help him up, but Travis stayed down.

Minutes later, Jessica, Kyra, and a few other girls walked out of the shadows.

Jessica looked disgusted. "I can't believe this," she said. "What a bunch of idiots."

Kyra ran over to Daniel and hugged him. Jessica walked toward Justin and slapped him.

"You of all people. Ganging up on Daniel. I thought you were different. You're just as bad as Travis," she said.

"Hey, watch the face," Justin said. He rubbed his cheek. It stung. "I was only here playing security," he added. "We were here to help Daniel. Who knew Daniel was a martial arts expert?"

Jessica blushed. "Oh. Well, I still can't see why you hang out with Travis," she said. "Daniel told Kyra he was coming here to talk to

Travis. He didn't tell Kyra what it was all about. She was worried so we decided to come out and see what was going on. When I saw you standing with Travis, I thought you were had a part in it."

"What do you care if I'm in on this or not?" Justin asked.

"Man, you really are thick," she answered. She brushed her long blond hair off her shoulder and walked closer to Justin. Then she stood on her tiptoes to whisper in his ear. "Why don't you call me later and we can talk about it?" she said quietly. She smiled, turned around, and walked away with some of the other girls.

Call me later? Justin thought. *Does Jessica actually like me?*

Travis got to his feet and rubbed his back. He walked around in the darkness for a while.

Daniel and Kyra walked through the Pizza Pit and stopped to talk by his car. Jessica left with the other girls. Dave and Jamal were planning on driving home. They offered Travis and Justin a ride. Travis looked embarrassed. He turned and started to walk home alone.

Justin walked around to the front of the restaurant. He wanted to tell Travis exactly what he thought of him, privately. He ran out to the parking lot and told Emily to head home. Then he ran over to catch up with Travis. He was walking along the train tracks that headed toward the school.

Justin was relieved that no one was getting beaten up that night. At least, that's what Justin thought.

chapter 18

turning the tables

Justin followed Travis as he walked down the tracks. The tracks were totally different at night than during the daytime. Justin tripped a few times on the railway ties.

There were no houses on either side of the tracks. Not even a street light shone through the darkness. The only light came from the moon. This, Justin thought, must have been what everyone called "the wrong side of the tracks." The two boys turned and started to cut through an alley to get to a street with some lights.

"Thanks for coming with me," Travis asked. "That was pretty bad. It's going to take more than just us to get him next time."

"Travis, when are you going to give it up?" Justin asked. He didn't care what Travis thought of him. He didn't want to hang out with him anymore. Besides, he missed being in the drama club. And he missed the good old days in John's toy room.

"You are rude to people, and treat them like crap. When you treated Kyra badly, you deserved to lose her. By the way, Mr. Thomas knows about the exam. He found my study notes. You have to rewrite the exam."

Travis groaned. "Oh great. I am going to be sent away for sure. Thanks a lot, Justin. Do you have any idea how hard it is to make my parents happy? I just keep on failing. It's not my fault. The move to Bayview was my last chance. My dad will seriously send me to military school."

He was trying to play the sympathy card. It wasn't going to work this time.

"You know what? It is your fault. You have everything, and you throw it away. Don't blame the world for your bad choices. Maybe military school would be good for you," Justin told him.

Travis stopped walking. "What did you say?" He looked angry. Justin thought Travis might just give him a beating after all.

They both stopped talking when they heard noises coming from the dark shadows. It sounded like footsteps coming down the alley.

When the sounds got close enough, Justin

could see that there were at least six guys walking toward them.

Justin gulped. They didn't look like the kind of guys you wanted to meet in a dark alley. As far as Justin could tell, they were about nineteen years old. Maybe a little older. They all had a small "s" tattooed on the side of their faces.

They stopped in front of Justin and Travis. Justin knew at once that they were a gang.

Oh no. We are going to get it, Justin thought.

They had just been behind the Pizza Pit, preparing for a fight with Daniel. Now, they were the ones being cornered. The only difference was, they were facing a real gang.

"Look at the good little high school boys," one of the guys said. He spit on the ground and walked toward Travis.

"Didn't your mommies tell you not to walk down dark alleys alone? This is our turf," the other one said. The other gang members started to laugh.

"So, what do you have for us? Money? We will be taking those jackets, thank you very much," the one with the buzz cut said. He had chains hanging from his belt loops.

"What else, boys? I see this one over here has some basketball shoes on that are just my size," one of the other guys said. "And look at the gold

watch. Looks like we have a little rich boy here."
He reached over and flicked Travis's head.

"Hand over your stuff. If you don't yell or fight back, we promise not to kill you," the guy with the buzz cut said. "I can't promise that there won't be a lot of blood, though. There's a quota for broken bones we still have to meet, though. I think we're a little short, don't you?" he asked the guys beside him. They laughed and nodded.

"Let's take the boots to them, guys," he said. Travis turned to cover his head with his arms. Justin's heart was beating a mile a minute. He looked around, but there was nowhere to run.

Justin panicked. He didn't know if he would leave that alley alive. He closed his eyes and waited for the feeling of pain.

All of a sudden they saw some headlights at the end of the alley. Everyone turned around to look. The car was driving slowly.

It pulled into the alley. Then it stopped in front of them with its headlights beaming into the darkness. Justin looked to see if it was a police car, but it wasn't. He hoped whoever it was wasn't going to drive away when they noticed that it was a gang in the alley. Most people would be afraid to get caught in the middle of a gang fight.

A door opened on the driver's side of the car. Someone yelled out, "Hey, we have a cell phone. The police are on their way."

The gang members stepped back a minute and looked at each other. Sirens were screaming somewhere in the distance.

"Travis, Justin, get in," the voice called. They ran toward the car, praying that the gang didn't follow them. Whoever was in the car knew their names. Justin normally wouldn't just jump into a strange car. The only other choice he had was to stay and get beaten in the alley.

The gang members ran the other way. They didn't want to take the chance that the police might actually show up.

Justin and Travis jumped into the open back door. They closed the door and hit the locks. And then Justin smiled.

Daniel turned around from the front seat and looked back. "Good thing I took this way home," he said. He drove off into the dark night.

glossary

alley
A narrow street between buildings

audience
A group of people who gather together
to watch a performance

bleachers
A set of benches that looks like a wide
set of stairs

detention
Being kept back after school for misbehavior

karate
A martial arts program

method acting
A type of acting whereby an actor uses
a character's thoughts and feelings to try
to "become" the character

Special Thanks

Tea Leaf Press gratefully acknowledges the help of Gary Osmond, Kerri Wall-Wilson, Ingrid Krahn, and the many other educators for their contribution of time, talent, and treasure. Their willingness to assist in making these books for children was truly inspiring.

Thank you to Ron Voth, Rick Fast, Daniel Fast, and the many other students who read entire manuscripts to help ensure the stories were interesting and accessible.

We give our most heartfelt thanks to our partners and families, who did everything from proofreading, printing, and collating to making sure that life at home continued to function. Your support was amazing. We would not have made it without you. Thank you to John Evoy, Ron Fast, Peter & Katie Fast, Peter Hough, Barbara & George Hough, Marj & Mike Levigne, Kevin Levigne, Leslie Perry, Ursula Sotzek, and Sam Turton.

Finally, we wish to extend a most sincere thank you to Ben Kooter and Vanwell Publishing for the opportunity to make our dream a reality.

Dangerous Rivals The biggest rowing event of the year is coming up. Bayview's rivalry with another high school gets out of control.

Muscle Bound Competition for sports is tough. Everyone is looking for an edge. How far is Kalen Sommers prepared to go?

After Dinner Barf There's a bad seed causing trouble at Bayview High. Fighting. Stealing. Starving. It's enough to make you want to throw up.

Dear Liz Liz Gordon agreed to write an advice column for the Bayview High newspaper. She never expected romance!

Beating Up Daniel Cool friends. Parties. Plans for a bloody beating. Justin has to make a decision. Will he become a target himself?

Check out our website for the latest at Bayview High

TEA
LEAF
PRESS